THE MERCY OF HUMANITY

The Mercy of Humanity

SHANTE R. CARTER

The Mercy of Humanity
Copyright © 2013 Shante Carter
ISBN 978-1-490498-40-9

Cover design by Latonya Hines
Interior design by Candy Abbott
Edited by Joyce Magnin, Fran D. Lowe, and Wilma Caraway

Published by Fruitbearer Publishing, LLC
P.O. Box 777, Georgetown, DE 19947
302.856.6649 • FAX 302.856.7742
www.fruitbearer.com • info@fruitbearer.com

Printed in the United States of America

DEDICATION

This book is dedicated to my mother and mother-in-law who went before me in their own publishing endeavors. You both showed me courage and determination.

Thank you to my husband, Aaron, for supporting me, uplifting me, and praying for me.

Zoe and Caleb, I thank you for inspiring and motivating me.

Daddy, Pops, and Selena, thank you for loving me.

CHAPTER 1

Stacey sat at her desk, in front of her bedroom window facing the forest that flanked her house. Feelings of both anxiety and excitement ran through her as she contemplated stepping out of her comfort zone. This would be a big step for her—attempting to do something she had never done before. Stacey was a controlling person who did not like inserting herself into arenas where she wasn't quite sure she would be successful. Writing a book was going to take a lot of time, hard work, patience, and diligence. Most of these things she struggled with on a regular basis. So how then would she be able to put them all in one and make this book thing work?

She stared at the blank screen on her laptop in wonder and angst. Her arms reached up into the air as she stretched and let out a long, slow breath. Looking out of the window, she cracked a smile at the images of all the different colors on the leaves. The beautiful view somehow calmed her, and she began typing on her computer.

Mercy is something that is not completely understood and reaches far beyond our psyche. It doesn't come naturally, I believe. You have to work hard at it, and it's a continuous process. I can look back over the years and see how mercy was extended to me here and there. Yet on my side of mercy, I was mostly consumed with selfishness, lack of understanding, and low self-esteem, so I couldn't see the bigger picture. I recently had the urge to dig deeper into this thing called mercy. I was so compelled that I had to write. I had to let it out so that it didn't consume me.

"Mom! Come on!" Riley bellowed from the bottom of the steps. It was time for her daughter to go to school, and Stacey was running late. She just wanted to get started because it felt so tangible and real. But with her daughter rushing her out of the house, it didn't seem as though she was going to get much done.

"Riley! I'll meet you in the car. Let me finish this, *please.*" Stacey sighed as she tried to recapture her thought process. When nothing came to her mind, she slammed the laptop shut in frustration. Why don't I ever get a moment to myself in my own house, where I pay the bills? I feel like they know when I'm trying to do something just for me. It's a conspiracy.

Stacey jumped up from her desk and grabbed her sweater from the corner of the bed as she walked out of her bedroom. Running down the steps, she shouted, "Let me grab my stuff, and I'll be right there!"

Walking into the kitchen, she was greeted by an impatient pre-teen with her hands on her hips. "Did you hear me say, 'I'll meet you in the car'?" Stacey asked. "I advise you to take your hands off your hips and find your way there."

Riley huffed as she stomped out of the house. "Now I know how my mom felt when I was a teenager. I need to send her some flowers and apologize or something," Stacey said, rolling her eyes as she gathered her things for work and headed to the car.

"I lost my train of thought, thank you very much," Stacey said as she slammed the car door shut. There was no response from the back seat. She turned around and noticed that Riley was wearing her headphones, blocking out her very existence. Her eyes were closed, head rocking, and fingers snapping.

"Oh, yeah!" Riley sang out as if she was giving her own concert. Her ponytail swung back and forth to the beat of the music.

Eyeing her daughter's hot pink shirt with "Princess" on the front and denim pants with matching hot pink shoes, Stacey smiled as she turned around to start the car. "Lawd, thank You for this child—her gifts, her purpose, and my nerves lasting through it all." She laughed at her short prayer of serenity, pulled out of her driveway, and headed toward Riley's school. The ride was quiet, giving Stacey time to reflect. *How in the world am I going to get all of this done? I have work, my family, my church—and now, this book? I'm not so sure—*

"Mom." Riley interrupted Stacey's thoughts once again. "I forgot to ask you if I could go to Kristine's house after school." She paused and waited for a response with a smile on her face.

"Okay," Stacey said.

"Okay, I can go?" Riley's voice peaked as she slowly took her ear buds out.

"You made a statement, Riley. You didn't ask me a question, so I just acknowledged what you said. Okay, I heard you."

"Ohh! Why do you always do that? You know what I mean!" Riley whined.

"Riley, you know I don't interpret your statements. If you have a question, then you should ask it," Stacey responded.

"Yes, I know. But don't you know what I mean?" Riley huffed and crossed her arms.

"Riley, Nana and Pop Pop raised me the same way. I see the effect it had on me in my life, and I appreciate them for it." She looked at Riley in the rearview mirror. "And trust me, one day you will too. Now, what is your question, sweetie?"

"May I go to Kristine's house after school?" Riley mumbled.

"Yes, you may go to Kristine's house until after I get off work, and I'll pick you up from there. I'll call her mother to make sure it's okay and confirm that she'll be home with you all," Stacey said.

"Thanks, Mom."

They pulled up to the school, and Stacey put the car in park. She turned around to speak to Riley. "Now, you know the expectations of your father and me and, most importantly, of the Lord, so govern—"

"Govern yourself accordingly. Yes, I know, Mom." Riley blew Stacey a kiss as she opened the door. "I love you today, Mom!" she said before shutting the door and running to catch up with her friends.

Stacey watched Riley for a moment before pulling off. "Okay, Lord. It's just You and me all the way to work." She resisted the urge to turn the radio on. In the silence, she could hear the fallen leaves crunching under her car tires as she headed down the street.

Stacey was a well-educated woman who worked as a marketing executive at a well-established advertising agency in downtown Chicago. She had been able to work her way up through the company and was now one of the few female top executives. She knew she was good at marketing, but writing this book was something new. Thinking about venturing into unknown territory began to unnerve Stacey. She wasn't used to having these feelings of inadequacy.

As Stacey sat at the stoplight, she looked around the neighborhood. She felt the beaming sun rays against her cheek as she looked up at the cloudless sky. She suddenly was overwhelmed and began to cry. Feeling insecurity rising inside of her, Stacey struggled to keep herself and her emotions under control.

"Are You sure You want me to do this? I mean, there are so many people who have done this before that may be better suited. Oh! Pastor's wife, Sister Brenda, has written several books, so she could probably knock this one out of the park. I . . . I really think I misunderstood You, Lord. You couldn't have meant me, right?" Stacey prayed aloud.

"Beep! Beep! Beep!" the car blasted behind her. Stacey drove off, wiping her tears. She decided to call her husband, even though she was smart enough to know that she had heard the right thing. She couldn't lie to herself or talk her way out of it. But she knew she was still scared, and her husband would be able to help. She pulled out her phone and Bluetooth and called her husband.

"Hey, honey. Did you make it to work already?"

Stacey was hoping he would say something comforting without her even having to tell him what was going on. Charles was the funniest man she knew. Besides her father, he was the most spiritual man she had met. He was also a great father to Riley. He had a way of knowing what Stacey needed by how she sounded and her attitude. They had been married for more than fifteen years, and outside of the normal bumps in the road, they had a great relationship. She didn't have time to go into the details of her issue. She was just looking for one of his famous jokes so she could laugh and get herself together before walking into her office.

"Babe, hey. I was just about to call you. You're not going to believe what Andrew showed me this morning. His wife bought him that new phone I was looking at the other day . . . just because." He cleared his throat with a slight chuckle underneath his breath.

"So, what I hear you saying is that you want me to call her and ask her to buy you the phone you were looking at the other day?" Stacey smiled as she waited for his comeback.

"Really? It's like that? Okay, I see what happens when I have to leave early for meetings. You don't get your fix, so then you get spicy. So, what I hear you saying is that I'll see you when I get home tonight for our meeting," Charles said.

"I think that will be the best way for us to really understand what each other is trying to say, honey," Stacey replied, laughing as she wiped the last of her tears away.

Her tone got serious. "No, really. I do need to sit down with you when we get home tonight. I have some things on my heart, and they're a bit overwhelming, so I need you to be my sounding board." Stacey started to feel better just by sharing that small bit of information.

"Okay, Stacey, whatever you need. Call me at work if you can't wait until tonight. You know I got you, girl." The strong tone in his voice sent a warming comfort through Stacey's body.

"How is it that your voice and words somehow always seem to make me feel like everything's going to be all right?" Stacey asked.

"'Cuz, I'm just that guy. I can't help it." Charles said sweetly.

"Ha, ha, ha. Well thank you, Boo! I love you today," Stacey said as she hung up the phone.

Stacey walked into her office a little distracted but ready to keep her day moving so she could get home. "Good morning, Brandi. Any calls for me?"

"No, Mrs. Brighton, and the only major thing on your calendar today is your afternoon meeting to present the ad campaign," her assistant said while handing her a large cup of soy vanilla latte from Starbucks.

"Thanks, Brandi," Stacey said with a smile as she took the coffee from Brandi's hand. She walked into her office, rested her briefcase on the couch and headed over to the window. She took a minute to sip her latte and look at the view of rush hour as she tried focusing her mind.

"Knock, knock. Stacey?" a voice called from the doorway.

Stacey swung around and smiled as she saw her friend standing in front of her. "Hey, Whitney. Wow! You look great! I need to get back to going to Pilates class with you."

"Aw, thanks, girl. And yes, you do. I'm lonely without you. We have a new teacher, and she is no joke. How's your day looking? You want to do lunch?"

Stacey welcomed the distraction, so she agreed. "That would be great. I have a two o'clock meeting, so let's go no later than 12:30." Stacey and Whitney were two of the very few African Americans at their company, so they hung together a lot. They worked out together, shopped together, and shared their mutual frustrations about work.

"Sounds good, but I hope you brought some flats because those pumps are hot but don't look like walking shoes," Whitney said, pointing to Stacey's shoes as she walked out the office. Stacey smiled and sat down at her desk. She began to work and attempted to stay focused, but her mind kept wandering to the book she was supposed to be writing.

"You want to sit outside?" Whitney asked as they carried their lunches on a tray at a nearby café.

"Um, I think I want to sit inside today," Stacey said as her hair blew in her face, sticking to her lip gloss.

"Oh! Okay," Whitney said, laughing. "See, girl, if you would just cut your hair off like me, you would be fine. But no, you want that long Beyoncé hair!"

"Whatever. I had this hair way before Beyoncé!" Stacey said, sitting down at an empty table. "So, how was your weekend?"

"Terrible." Whitney shook her head. "My boyfriend's ex-girlfriend all of a sudden moved to Chicago. She was calling him all weekend, asking for his help with this and that. I trust him, but I don't trust her. She said she's moved on, but I don't believe her."

"Girl, I wouldn't trust her either. Don't even give her an inch because I can guarantee she'll take a mile." Stacey shook her fork at Whitney as she sternly proclaimed her opinion.

"Well, that's what I told Matt, but he believes her," Whitney complained.

"Well, you need to lay it on the line and let him know that for your relationship it's not going to work, so he needs to make a decision. Trust me, you won't regret it," Stacey warned.

"Wow, you seem to be really passionate about this. Is there something you're not telling me?" Whitney probed.

"Huh? Me? No, I . . . um . . . I just have a feeling," Stacey stumbled. "Girl, just keep me posted. Now, tell me about this new Pilates teacher. I think I'm going to start back up next week," Stacey said, quickly changing the subject. Whitney didn't seem to mind the change in topic, so they continued making small talk through lunch and headed back to work.

"Brandi, I'm headed to the meeting. Please bring the laptop in so we can present the campaign," Stacey said as she walked toward the conference room. She sat at the back of the room as the meeting began. She was doing her best at keeping focused while her boss spoke; but as she sat, words just started flowing into her mind, and she started scribbling. She wrote two pages of notes, phrases, and thoughts until she heard her name being repeated.

"Stacey, Stacey. Earth to Stacey. Can you give your final overview of the ad campaign before we send it to the client?" Her boss stared at her note pad. The look on his face quickly brought Stacey back to reality. She swallowed hard and snapped out of her daze.

She sat up straight in her chair and began to speak. "Oh . . . oh, yes . . . um, I actually have a PowerPoint presentation that I wanted to share in regards to that. Let me just . . ." As she scrambled to regroup, she thought to herself, *Lord please keep me focused and help me balance all of this with my responsibilities.*

She looked around the conference room at all the faces staring back at her. Tugging nervously at her suit jacket, she cleared her throat and stood up from her chair, then walked quickly over to the projector screen. She nodded to Brandi, who was sitting at her laptop, ready to navigate through the PowerPoint slides. Stacey began her presentation and got herself back on track. After the presentation was complete, she looked at her boss and said, "I really put a lot of effort into this one, Chris. I've researched the client and their past ad campaigns, and I really believe it will take their product to the next level."

"Great job, Stacey. I really think this is going to seal the deal for our team." He gave her a thumbs-up as he left the room. "Okay everybody, keep me posted and let's reconvene next week."

As everyone left the room, Stacey plopped down in the chair and rolled her eyes. "Whew!" She exhaled and gathered her notes. The end of the day couldn't come soon enough.

CHAPTER 2

The daily routine of picking up Riley, making dinner, and helping with homework felt especially slow on this particular day for Stacey. She just wanted to clock out and talk through this thing with Charles. She was so excited to share what she sensed God was asking her to do. Charles had always known what his purpose was and where he was headed. Yet for Stacey it hadn't always been so clear. She would invest in other people and their dreams, but as for her own, she allowed the fear of the unknown and self-doubt to hinder her. This time seemed different. Everything was so clear that it was as if God was yelling at her. She knew she had an uphill battle, but she believed she could really do it.

"Riley, please finish cleaning the kitchen for me. I need to talk to your dad about some stuff." Stacey handed Riley the dish towel and nodded toward the sink full of dishes.

"Mom! Ewww!" Riley covered her ears with her wrists, squeezed her elbows together, and closed her eyes. She was used to seeing affection between her parents, and it always "grossed" her out. She knew which words were used as a code between her parents, so she automatically assumed Stacey was talking about sex.

"Calm down, girl. This is a real conversation. And for the record, when a man and a woman are married, it's a beautiful thing when they come together as one. You need to say 'ewww' instead to all that nasty stuff on TV and in the movies."

Stacey walked past Charles and gave him a high-five. "Hello, somebody!" Charles grabbed Stacey in his arms and dipped her like a dancer, kissing her passionately. They both laughed as Riley ran out of the room and they headed upstairs.

"Okay, hon'. What's on your mind? You had me wondering all day what this was about," Charles said. He followed Stacey through the double doors of their bedroom, closing them slowly behind him.

"You think you were distracted today? I was a *mess.*" Stacey threw her hands up in the air as she fell back onto the loveseat in their sitting room.

Charles lit the fireplace and sat down on the floor in front of her, resting his head on her knees.

Stacey let out a sigh before speaking. "I'm sure you'll find this shocking, but . . . I'm writing a book."

Charles lifted his head and looked at Stacey. "A book?"

"Yes, a book. I've been dreaming about it lately, and I prayed to God, asking Him what it meant. He said to write a book. I really feel like I heard Him correctly, Charles."

"Well, okay then. What's it going to be about?" Charles asked.

"It's about mercy. Over the past few years, in going through the normal things in life, I've been hurt." Stacey shifted in her seat nervously. "And through that hurt I've been forced to seek God for healing. The more I sought Him, the more mercy I received and the more mercy I was compelled to give." Stacey smiled as she reached out for Charles' hand. "I feel like those life experiences are what God wants me to share with the world."

Charles kissed her hand gently. "Stacey, that's great. I'm truly excited for you. I would never have thought writing a book was on your purpose agenda. But hey, I know you can do anything you set your mind to, so I'm excited! Have you started writing?"

"A little. I mean, lately I've been absolutely consumed with the thought of it. I mean, actual words and phrases for the book are pouring out of my mind, and I can't contain myself. It literally feels like I'm going to burst. I couldn't even pay attention in my meeting today! Chris called on me to speak, and I was zoned out!"

"Wait a minute now, babe. You can't go losin' your job. You and Riley eat way too much for us to go down to one income." Charles stared at her with a serious look on his face.

"*Hush,* Charles." Stacey smacked his arm, and he pulled her to the floor.

Charles kissed her on the cheek and looked her in the eye. "You were created with a purpose, and it's truly a gift to actually realize what that purpose is. And to go after that purpose in spite of your fears is commendable. You can do this, and you have my utmost support. I'll do whatever you need me to do to help you get this done. We can talk through it, I'll type for you, or if I have to . . . relax you."

He smiled and kissed her again. "I believe in you, and I know Riley does too, babe, so don't worry. You can be as vulnerable as you need to be with us because we'll take care of you."

Stacey exhaled. "Thank you . . . really, thank you. I know all of that, but hearing you say it means so much more. I really am excited and terrified at the same time." Stacey jumped up from the floor and began walking toward the bathroom. "I think I'm going to take a bath and relax. This has been a very exhausting day." As she walked away, Charles reached out and grabbed her leg.

"Can I come? My day was exhausting, too." She smiled and nodded her head. They spent the rest of the evening bathing and loving each other by candlelight.

By that next weekend Stacey was really feeling the "author thing." She had gone out and purchased her writing materials and started putting some of her ideas and thoughts together. As she sat in bed early Saturday morning, she pressed Charles to listen to her read some of her writings.

"Charles. Charles! *Listen!* What do you think of this?" Stacey had a note pad in one hand and was shaking her husband with the other as he attempted to ignore her. "Wake up, honey!" she shouted.

"It's Saturday," Charles mumbled from beneath the down comforter. "Come back in an hour."

"Come *on,* babe. I'm too excited to sleep! I'm an author, and I have words to share with you." Stacey smiled as she started to pull the covers back off of him.

It was fall, so there was just enough chill to get his attention, especially since their fire from the night before had burned out.

Charles shot up and glared at Stacey. He sat there and rubbed his eyes. "Are you wearing reading glasses?" Stacey nodded yes with a very serious look on her face. "Stace, you have 20/20 vision. Why do you have glasses on?"

She smiled and said, "They go with my new purpose . . . what?"

He tilted his head and stared at her.

"Okay, *okay.*" She laughed as she took the glasses off and put them on the nightstand. "But I really want you to hear this and tell me what you think. Then you can go back to sleep—I promise."

Charles nodded and gestured for her to go on with her reading. "Okay, it's not much; but it's what I have so far, so don't be too hard."

"Just read," Charles snapped.

"All *right,* then." She cleared her throat. "In order to really be able to administer mercy, you must first allow the Most High God to reveal His perfect mercy to you. Once that mercy is displayed in your life, only then will you truly be able to administer your mercy—" Charles started shifting in the bed.

"What? You don't like it?" Stacey's voice squeaked.

"Okay. Well, let me first say that I truly believe God has birthed this dream of you writing a book. I also believe that He has equipped you with the talents and skills to write the book. And these talents and skills have been within you since He formed you in your mother's womb. Therefore, they have been lying dormant for a long time now . . ."

Stacey started to glare back at her husband as he continued his long-winded attempt to tell her that her excerpt was bad.

"Charles! Get to the point!" Stacey started to sound irritated.

"Look, babe. I think maybe you should go to a writing class to see how people organize their thoughts and decide on a writing style. You just need to get a clearer understanding of how the whole thing works. I get what you're trying to say in what you just read. It just isn't—"

Stacey jumped up out of the bed and cut him off. "Okay, thanks for your help. I have some errands to run. I'll see you later." She ran into the bathroom and slammed the door.

"Well, can I at least get a kiss for waking up out of my comfortable Saturday morning sleep and listening to you?" Charles begged.

The bathroom door flew open. Stacey stomped over to the bay window and flung the curtains open, letting the bright fall sunshine into their bedroom. "That's cold, Stace. That's cold." She walked into the bathroom with a smirk on her face as Charles buried his head under the covers.

Stacey loved fall weekends because she could put on jeans, a T-shirt, and a cardigan sweater. Her weekdays were filled with suits, heels, and makeup, so dressing down on the weekend was a treat. This particular Saturday she decided to throw on a sweat suit and some tennis shoes.

"You may be cold, but you sure are *fine*, girl." Charles said with his eyes peeking over the comforter as Stacey headed out the room. She looked back over her shoulder at him and winked.

Stacey headed down the hall to her daughter's room. "Riley?" Stacey opened the bedroom door and slipped her head in. "Are you coming with me today? I have some errands to run in the city."

"Sure, Mom. Can Keisha come with us?" Riley asked.

Stacey rolled her eyes. "That girl is loud, Ry Ry, and I'm not sure if I want all of that today. I have a lot on my mind, and I just want to flow with what I have to do."

"You know Keisha is having issues at home, so getting her out of the house would be good for her right now," Riley said as she sat in her pajamas in the middle of her bed, taking out the pin curls in her hair. "That's fine. I'll just stay home and hang out with her here," Riley snapped as she jumped out of the bed and walked past her mother, almost pushing her aside.

"Little girl, you are free to not like what I say, but don't take it too far," Stacey said, turning around and watching Riley walk to the bathroom. "You may be almost as tall as I am, but I am still your mother, and I will knock you out old-school style."

"Sorry, Mom. She's my best friend, and I want to help her. I'll just stay here, okay?" she said, leaning against the wall with her arms crossed.

"Best friend . . . those come and go," Stacey mumbled.

"What does that mean?" Riley frowned.

"Nothing, sweetie . . . Um, I'll see you when I get home later." Stacey immediately felt badly about her comment. She walked over to Riley and kissed her forehead. "I think it's very nice that you want to be there for your best friend. I'm proud of you." She hugged Riley and turned to go downstairs.

Stacey walked into the kitchen and headed straight for the coffee pot. She felt uneasy about what she had just said to Riley. *I'm just jumpy because of all this book energy,* she said to herself as she opened the cabinet to get a coffee mug. As she poured her coffee, she spoke aloud. "Stacey, calm down. It's not a big deal. She doesn't even know what you were talking about. Leave the past in the past." She turned on the small TV in the corner, sat down on the barstool, and distracted herself with the weekend news.

CHAPTER 3

"I'm headed out," Stacey shouted as she washed out her mug in the sink and headed toward the garage door.

"Bye, Mom! See you later!" Riley yelled from her room. Charles didn't make a sound, indicating he was still buried under the covers.

As Stacey rode down her driveway toward the street, she squinted her eyes and stuck her hand in her purse, feeling around for her sunglasses. The bright sunshine created a glare on her windshield. The morning air was brisk but not too cold, so she drove with her windows cracked open. She smiled as she listened to the radio and drove toward downtown without any traffic. The city, usually filled with the hustle and bustle of the week, was quiet and inviting.

She parked her car and ventured into some of her favorite stores re-stocking her must-have items. As she walked down the street, she felt the cool breeze on her face. The leaves had started to fall, and all the colors of the season were strategically displayed in the store windows on the mannequins. The fashions seemed to call her name.

Everything she saw was indicating the change in season. It seemed to be a perfect time for a new season in her life. She started to feel inspired and excited all over again about her book.

Stacey made her way into a clothing store. "May I help you?" a very short saleswoman asked. She was shorter than Riley and had red hair and freckles. Stacey, thrown off a little, tried not to smile too hard.

"Oh, I'm fine. I'm just looking." Stacey turned away so she wouldn't embarrass herself or the saleswoman.

"Okay. Well, let me know if you need anything," she said as she walked away.

"Actually . . . um, excuse me." Stacey reached out for the woman. "I'm looking for that sweater that's in the display window. It's absolutely gorgeous, and I want to get it."

"Yes, we just got that in, and it's been selling like hotcakes. What color and size do you need?"

"Let me see. I think I would like the green and black in a medium." Stacey cupped her chin in her hand as she tried to make her decision. "No . . . can I get the white one as well?"

"Please make up your mind, lady," a voice rang out from behind Stacey.

Before Stacey could turn around with an attitude, she recognized that voice. She put her hand on her hip as she slowly turned around to face her antagonist. "Lady, can you mind your own business? I'm trying to make a transaction here," she said before she started laughing and hugging the woman. "Charlene, what are you doing here?"

"Girl, I'm running around just like you. I saw you from the window, so I came in to bother you," she said, smiling.

"Is everything okay, ma'am?" the saleswoman asked from behind them.

Charlene and Stacey looked at each other and smiled. "Yes, this is my very good friend. She's crazy, but she won't hurt anyone," Stacey replied.

"Oh, okay. I'll get your sweaters and hold them at the register when you're ready to check out."

"Thanks, I'll be right over." Stacey watched the woman walk away and then whispered to Charlene, "You're taller than she is. I didn't think that was possible."

"Ha, ha, ha. Very funny, Stacey." Charlene pinched Stacey on her arm. "I'm actually glad I ran into you. I was going to call you later because we need to strategize about those teens tomorrow during Sunday school."

"Yes, we need to be ready, and when I say we, I mean you." Stacey glared at Charlene.

"Yes, girl. I'm ready for them this time. I've reviewed the Sunday school notes, and I'm ready! Now who am I going to be this week? Good cop or bad cop?" Charlene looked genuinely excited about her question. She placed her hands on her hips as she waited.

"Charlene, you know you don't do well with the bad-cop role. Most of the kids are bigger than you, so you overcompensate. You always try and talk through your teeth to sound mean, but it just makes the kids laugh. Just leave it to me, okay?" Stacey laughed.

"I don't know if I appreciate your rude comment, Stacey. I don't agree with you. Israel Houghton said I know who I am, so I don't need you to tell me, thank you very much." She was shaking her finger and her neck with a smirk on her face.

"Okay lady, whatever you say. Look, I have a hair appointment in ten minutes. I'm going to call you when I slow down so we can do lunch. Are you free later? Stacey asked. I have something exciting I want to talk to you about."

"Sure. Let's just meet at Hogan's around 2:30. We can also discuss the whole cop thing a little more because, frankly, I don't know what you're trying to say." Charlene gave Stacey smooches as she walked away.

"Girl, don't act like you don't know what I'm talking about!" Stacey shouted as Charlene walked away. "Okay, you can be the bad cop, but you're going to be mad at me when I'm laughing with the kids tomorrow." Stacey shook her head and laughed as she walked to the register to pay for her sweaters.

Stacey left the store and walked a few blocks to the hair shop. It was filled with weekend customers as she made her way to the front desk to sign in. Stacey loved going to the salon to get away and relax. The hardwood floors, brightly lit hair stations, soothing music and aromas, and most of all, the great customer service made her drive into the city worthwhile.

THE MERCY OF HUMANITY

"Hey, Stacey. It's been a while since we've seen you in here." The owner welcomed her and led her to the back to get started. "Hang up your coat here, and head over to the shampoo bowl. We're ready for you."

"Thanks, Kim. I know it's been a while. I've been so busy with work and the family that I've been neglecting my alone time here at the shop."

Stacey looked around to see if her stylist had come in. She caught her eye and smiled. "Ahhhh, Lynn, my hair is very excited to see you." As she walked back to the shampoo bowl, she saw a few of her friends. "Hey, Cathy and Maureen! Long time, no see."

"Hey, Stacey! It's good to see you." Cathy said as she leaned back in the sink to get her hair washed.

"How did you know it was me, Cathy? You can't even see me without your glasses," Stacey said, laughing.

"We saw you when you came in," Maureen interjected.

"Maureen, I see you're back to the blonde hair. I really like it." Stacey smiled.

"Thanks, girl. I'm back to my pre-pregnancy size, so I needed my pre-pregnancy hair." Laughter erupted in the back of the salon.

"Stacey, I'm ready for you at this bowl." Lynn pointed to the middle shampoo bowl against the wall. Stacey sat down in the shampoo chair, leaned back, and started talking with the girls about what had been happening over the last few months.

"I'm gonna let this conditioner sit for a minute. I'll be right back, okay?" Lynn patted Stacey's shoulder.

"That's fine, thanks," Stacey said as she sat up to join in her girlfriends' conversation.

"So I told her that I was tired of reaching out to her and not getting any response in return. I can't keep giving to someone who doesn't want to give back," Maureen complained.

Stacey listened intently because there were always some good conversations at the shop. Now that she was doing research for her book, she figured this was the perfect opportunity to gather some information.

"I mean, am I supposed to just sit there and let her treat me any old kind of way?" Maureen said. "That's not how friends operate. I know she's going through a lot right now, but I can't be pulled and pushed at her command. What do you all think?"

Stacey's ears perked up. She had been rocking back and forth, waiting for a way to enter the conversation—just as if she was jumping double-dutch. Stacey cleared her throat, smiling at her friend. She waved at her to get her attention.

"Well, Maureen, I've come to realize that sometimes we have to look beyond ourselves and extend mercy toward others." Stacey could feel herself getting excited. "I mean, I personally have had to step back and look at the root issue and really see how I could take myself out of the picture and deal with what my friend needed." Maureen turned her head to the side and frowned. Stacey quickly finished her statement. "I mean, I know it's hard to feel like you've been taken for granted, but in the end it's not about you. It's about what the other person needs. That's how we show God's love to one another."

"So, you're saying that I should give all of me and expect nothing in return? Stacey, not even you can do that, girl," Maureen snapped, rolling her neck and waving her hands.

"No, I'm not saying that. I'm just saying that you have to set your own boundaries and not take it personal. Examine what they need and try to meet every need that you can. If those needs compromise you, your family, or your spiritual walk, then they are out of the question."

Cathy sat up from the bowl and nodded her head in agreement. "But if God gives us brand new mercies every single day even though we haven't given as much as we could, then how can we deny one of our friends a little more mercy?" The whole shampoo area seemed to be caught up in Stacey's speech, and she loved every moment of it. She couldn't wait to get home and write down the words she was sharing for her book. *Let's see what Charles thinks of this,* she thought to herself.

"Well, that does sound like the right thing to do. Leave it to you, Stacey, to get all deep on us." Maureen laughed as her shampoo girl called her to the next station.

"Girl, you know how you have a topic on your mind, and it comes up everywhere you go?" Stacey asked. "That's what's going on with me now. I'm researching mercy, so I see it in every situation nowadays." Lynn walked back to wash the conditioner out of Stacey's hair. As she laid her head back in the bowl, the women continued talking.

"It was good seeing you, Stacey," Cathy said as she stood up to go to her hairdresser's station.

"You too, Cathy. We have to get together soon. We all had so much fun last time, I can't wait to do something again," Stacey said as Lynn wrapped a warm towel around her hair.

"Yes," Maureen chimed in from across the salon. "I believe it's my turn. Charlene outdid herself last time, so I probably won't top her, but we'll still have fun."

Stacey gathered her things as she left the shampoo area. "Yes, she did. She just can't help herself. I'm actually meeting her at Hogan's after I leave here, so I'll let her know. Okay guys, I'll send you all some dates next week." She grinned as she sat in Lynn's chair and pulled out a magazine.

"Comfortable?" Lynn asked.

"Girl, yes. I'm just going to let you do your magic while I relax and catch up on some reading. I'm so busy at work and with the family that I miss out on the little things." Stacey sat back and let Lynn do whatever she wanted.

With her hair styled and feeling pampered, Stacey left the shop for lunch. She walked down the street to Hogan's and looked around for Charlene as she entered the restaurant.

"May I help you, ma'am?" the hostess asked. Stacey located Charlene in the back of the restaurant by the window.

"No, I found her. Thanks." She walked briskly to the back. She overflowed with excitement and was eager to share with her dear friend.

Years of fond memories flooded Stacey as she moved toward Charlene. Growing up together in Virginia, Stacey felt like Charlene was family. Even though Charlene moved to Chicago before Stacey did, got married, and had two kids, Charlene and Stacey stayed close and were always able to share their stories and issues with no judgment. They could tell each other the truth even when it was hard. Even though they fought like sisters, they always made up after they cooled down. Stacey's heart beat with anticipation at the thought of sharing her book idea with Charlene, the only other person besides Charles she was ready to tell.

Charlene stood up to greet Stacey. "Your hair is amazing! I really need to see Lynn as soon as possible. This mane of mine is roaring out of control."

Stacey stepped back and raised her eyebrows. "Oh, Charlene, you get cornier and cornier every day," Stacey said as she leaned in and hugged Charlene. "So, how are you feeling after your wonderful vacation last month? We haven't been able to catch up since you got back." They sat down at the table as the waiter poured water into their glasses.

"It was absolutely breathtaking. Tim and the kids and I had such a great time. We went to the beach every day, the kids had their own activities they could go to, and Tim and I spent a lot of quality time together." Charlene slammed her hand on the table and leaned in toward Stacey. "We really needed it. It's been a hectic time for us with the business expanding, and that time away really got us back on track." Charlene was glowing with excitement.

"Okay, girl. Let me find out you came home with another baby on the way," Stacey teased.

"Stacey, don't make me leave you sitting at this table alone today. It would be a shame for you to have to eat all by yourself because of your mouth!" Charlene shook her finger at Stacey.

"All right, then. You don't have to get all uptight, *Mom.* How about I just tell you what I came here to talk to you about? Can we talk about that?" Stacey raised her eyebrows and stared at Charlene, waiting for her to go ahead.

"Are you ready to order?" the waiter interrupted.

"Oh yes, I'll have the Cobb salad," Stacey said quickly.

"And I'll have the salmon with broccoli," Charlene said. "Can you make sure they cook that in as little butter as possible? I don't need all the extra calories."

"Sure, ma'am. No problem," the waiter said as he took their menus and walked away.

"I was waiting for the extra instructions," Stacey said sarcastically.

"Oh, really? Well, we all aren't blessed to have the perfect size 8 body, missy." Charlene rolled her eyes.

"Um, please. I work out four times a week." Stacey said.

"You're crazy, girl. Just tell me what you want to tell me." Charlene shook her napkin at Stacey, hurrying her along.

"Okay. Seriously, I'm so excited to share with you where God is taking me in my life!" Charlene extended her hand as if to say, "Go ahead." "About a month ago I dreamed I had written a book. I have never in my life thought about writing, so it was pretty weird to me. I kinda brushed it off until recently because I've just been consumed with words and thoughts for the book."

"Wow, that sounds exciting!" Charlene jumped in.

"I prayed about it, and I really believe it's an idea from God. I know He wants me to do this, Charlene. So I'm going to *write a book!*" She threw her hands up in the air and stared at Charlene.

"Oh, my goodness!" Charlene shouted. Realizing she was yelling, she whispered, "That's extremely exciting news, Stacey! Wow! Give me a hug." The women stood up and Charlene threw her arms around Stacey, rocking her back and forth.

Sitting down, Charlene let out a quiet scream. "Remember last year at the women's conference at our church? That's all they talked about—walking out your purpose."

"You're right. I remember that, but I had no idea that my purpose would be this. Charlene, I've been so overwhelmed. I know this is from God, and He'll give me everything I need to do it, but it seems like so much. I don't know how it will all get done." Stacey's smile slowly faded as she confessed her fears. "I can admit that I would normally run away from a challenge like this, but something is drawing me in." Sharing and speaking her dream out loud seemed to accentuate her fears.

"But you know that when you can't see how it's going to work out, it just means your testimony will be that much greater, right?" Charlene said, trying to encourage Stacey. "What will this book be about?"

Stacey's smiled returned. "Mercy. I want to share some of my experiences from those times I've been hurt. I want to walk the readers through my healing process and show them how mercy fits into the big picture."

"Sounds interesting, Stacey," Charlene said.

"I mean, you go through so much in life, and the more people you meet, the more opportunities you have to be hurt. I really think it will help people with forgiveness and moving forward in life," Stacey replied.

"Wow, that really shows maturity—to open up about what you have been through, your personal pain and the lessons learned. That's awesome." Suddenly Charlene's tone changed. "So you're going to include your experience with Kelly in there, right? Because that would—"

"And . . . oh, my goodness!" Stacey said. "Guess what happened in the shop today! Maureen started sharing her story about an issue with one of her friends. I was able to share about mercy and how it would help the situation, and she really listened. I was able to help her and get some material for my book." She smiled real big, hoping Charlene would let her last comment go.

Being the friend she was, Charlene obliged. "I'm absolutely inspired by you, Stacey. Allowing God to work through you and being totally vulnerable to something new takes courage."

They continued to talk about the book, Charlene's vacation, and their good cop/bad cop roles for Sunday school as they ate lunch. "Oh, Maureen and Cathy want to get together soon. I told them I would give them some dates next week, so let me know when you're free," Stacey mentioned as they stood to leave.

"Sounds great. I'll let you know," Charlene replied as they hugged goodbye. As Stacey began to let go, Charlene hugged her a little tighter. Stacey knew why she was hugging her but wasn't ready to go there. She smiled as they let go and began to walk toward the door.

"I'll see you tomorrow, bad cop," Stacey smirked.

"Whatever. You all will see that Charlene don't play come Sunday school tomorrow!" The women laughed as they walked to their cars to go home.

CHAPTER 4

Stacey spent the next few weeks researching how to write books, exploring the ideas and themes about mercy, and reading through her old journals to capture some more real-life experiences.

"I'm going to go do some writing," Stacey said one evening after dinner.

"Okay, babe. Let me know if you need something," replied Charles.

Stacey had a lot of ideas written down, but nothing was flowing in the form of what she considered to be a book. She sat down at the desk in their home office and opened her laptop. She stared at the screen, down at her notes, and then back to the screen. She repeated the confusing routine for a few minutes until she was frustrated.

"Grrrrr!" she growled at the computer screen. "Is this supposed to be this hard?" she asked, looking up at the ceiling.

Charles was walking by the office as Stacey conversed with God out loud. "Everything okay, babe?" he said, sticking his head in.

"Yeah . . . I mean, no." She leaned back, resting her head on the back of the chair.

"Can I help?" Charles asked, kissing her forehead from behind her chair.

"I just have all these ideas and great points, but I have no idea how to put them together. I mean, look at the screen." She pointed to the computer in front of her without looking up. "It's blank. I don't know about this, Charles. Maybe it's not the right time or something. I should be working on this ad campaign for J&J Publishing. Maybe I'll just do that tonight."

"This is your book time. Work is over, and it will be there in the morning," Charles said, walking around in front of Stacey and sitting on the edge of the wooden desk. "Have you thought about my idea of taking a writing class?" Stacey sat up and looked Charles squarely in the eyes. "Now, babe, just hear me out. You're the best at what you do in the advertising game. You went to school for that, so why not go to school for writing?"

"I don't know, Charles. I feel like I should just know what I am doing since God told me to do this. Shouldn't He just give me what I need?" Stacey stood up and walked over to the window, staring at the rain outside.

"That sounds like pride, Stacey."

Stacey spun around toward Charles. "Excuse me? Pride? How about faith?"

"Well, you could be right. Have you prayed about it, or are you making this assessment on your own?" Charles asked, walking over toward Stacey. He reached out to touch her arm, but she pulled away.

"Okay, thanks," she said, turning back around to look out the window.

"So, is this your way of starting a fight? I came in here to help, but now you're giving me attitude by not letting me touch you?" Charles backed away from Stacey and crossed his arms.

"What? This is not about you, Charles. Not everything is about you. You think you know everything and have the answer to everything. Please let me just figure this out on my own. I don't need you to rescue me from everything," Stacey shouted as she walked past Charles out of the office. She walked into the kitchen and opened the pantry door.

Charles followed her into the kitchen. "You will not take your frustrations out on me, woman." Charles said, closing the pantry door and looking Stacey in the eye. She couldn't look at him because she knew she was wrong. But she felt so much anger at her own inadequacies that she didn't let up.

"I am not taking anything out on you, Charles. But you always want to be the know-it-all. You want to give the right answers and have me do whatever you suggest. Well, all I'm saying is to let me handle this, please. You don't know anything about what God has for me to do or what I have prayed for." She put her hand on her hip and kept scolding Charles. "Did I even ask you to come into the office? I told you that this was my time alone to work on the book and asked for your support. That is all I asked, and this is what I get?"

Charles lowered his head in frustration and gritted his teeth. "I can't believe I let you bait me into this stupid fight," he said, laughing. He looked up at Stacey and leaned in close to her face. "*FINE!* I'm done helping you with your book." He turned to walk away. "Oh, and thanks for the lesson on mercy," he said while marching up the stairs. "I'm learning so much already."

Stacey stomped back to the office and flopped down on the couch. *He just doesn't understand what I'm going through,* she thought to herself. She sat there, staring at the empty screen on the desk for a minute, then jumped up, walked over to the desk, and slammed the laptop closed. She leaned over to turn off the lamp and left the office to go upstairs to bed.

Charles was getting into bed as she walked into the room. She paused at the doorway, ready to apologize.

"What?" Charles snapped.

"Nothing!" she snapped back as she closed the bedroom door. She silently walked over to the closet and began changing her clothes. She sat down on the edge of the bed with her back toward Charles, contemplating what to say. But then his words started to replay in her head and got her even angrier. She swung her feet around onto the bed, laid down, and went to sleep without saying a word.

The next morning the sun peeked through the curtains, waking up Stacey. She slowly opened her eyes and saw that Charles was not lying next to her. She turned over to look at the clock. Seeing that it was still early, she sat up in the bed and peeked around the corner into the closet. "Charles?" she asked quietly.

"He left already," Riley said as she walked past the bedroom door. "He said he had an early meeting."

"Oh," Stacey muttered.

"He said to tell you he has a busy day, and he'll see you tonight!" Riley shouted before shutting her bedroom door.

Stacey pulled the covers up to her neck as she felt a chill in the room. *I blew it,* she thought. "I hate when I do that!" she said out loud. She opened her nightstand drawer and pulled out a black notebook and a pen. She pulled her hair back into a ponytail and tied it in a bun. She slowly opened the book and began to write.

Dear Diary,

I've done it again. I know I promised that I wouldn't push Charles away like this, but I couldn't help it. I mean, we had so many good sessions with Dr. Briggs that, I must admit, I am disappointed in myself that I let it happen again. I will say that Charles has done his fair share, but last night he wasn't the issue. I was. I haven't written to you in a long time, and maybe that's the problem. I think I'm getting better, but it's still a journey. Or at least that's what Dr. Briggs says. I'll make it up to him. I just am so out of my comfort zone here that I just don't know what to do. What should I do, diary? Did I just ask you what I should do?

Beep! Beep! Beep! The alarm started blaring. Stacey closed her journal and turned off the alarm. She got out of bed and headed to the bathroom. Looking in the mirror, she spoke to herself. "You can do this, Stacey. Just get up and get moving, and everything will fall into place. Charles will come home tonight. Just give him space. Trust him. Love him."

Stacey got dressed and took Riley to school before heading to work. She stood in front of the elevator in the lobby of her office building, staring into space.

"Are you going to push the button?" a voice spoke next to her.

Stacey turned her head to see her boss. "Oh, morning, Chris. I was just daydreaming. I thought I pushed it." She smiled as she quickly pushed the up button. "I was wondering why it was taking so long." She laughed nervously.

"Rough morning?" he asked.

Stacey lowered her head. "Hmm, I guess you can say that." She caught herself and immediately stood up straight and looked him in the eye. "But I am definitely focused and will be working hard on the J&J Publishing campaign today. We're going to knock their socks off!"

"I know we will. I'm not worried, Stacey," he said as he motioned her to go into the elevator. "Ladies first." The elevator filled with people, and the ride up to the sixteenth floor was silent, much to Stacey's delight.

As Stacey walked by her assistant on her way into her office, she said, "Brandi, I'm going to be working hard on the J&J Publishing campaign this morning before the team meeting we have this afternoon. So please only interrupt me if it's an emergency. You know how I am when I get in my zone."

After shutting the door behind her, Stacey began to pray as she unpacked her briefcase, "Lord, I need you today. I recognize I am nothing—"

The door opened behind her, stopping her prayer in mid-sentence.

"Your coffee, Mrs. Brighton?" Brandi asked as she held out the cup.

"Thank you, Brandi," Stacey replied, walking over to grab her drink. As she turned away, she stopped and looked over her shoulder. "Brandi?"

"Yes, ma'am?" Brandi leaned into the office with her hand on the doorknob.

"Good morning."

"Thank you. Good morning to you, too," Brandi said, shutting the door gently.

Stacey sat down at her desk and logged in. She read her e-mails and tried to begin working on her ad campaign. But all she could think about was her fight last night with Charles.

She opened the Internet and Googled writing classes at Evanston Community College. She searched the website, looking for something that seemed to fit her. Finally, she found a course title that interested her: "Fundamentals of Literary Writing 101." Stacey read aloud the course description. "This is an introduction to the writing process. Students will learn how to research and gather information for the purpose of writing a book. By the end of the course, students should be able to outline and create chapters for a book in order to set the stage for the composition of a story."

"What's going on in here?" Chris demanded, walking into Stacey's office.

"Huh?" Stacey jumped. "Oh, Chris, you scared me. I . . . I was just working on the campaign, of course," Stacey said, clicking her mouse to get rid of the site she was looking at.

"I thought I heard you reading something about writing a story?" he asked, sitting in the chair in front of Stacey's desk.

"Yes, a story. I mean, half of these presentations are about telling a story, so I was just doing some research." She knew he wouldn't care about her being online; she just didn't want to share with him what she was doing.

"Great idea! See, that's why I keep you on my team. You're always stepping outside the box," Chris said as he winked at Stacey.

"Thanks, Chris. You also keep me because I meet your deadlines so . . ." Stacey smiled to let him know she was trying to work.

"Oh, yes! I came in to let you know that some of us are going out tonight, and I was wondering if you would like to join us."

He leaned forward and whispered, "It's on the company." As he reclined in the chair, he continued, "And you don't usually come out with us, Stacey. It really is a networking thing. I know you want to move up in the company, so you should probably try and make it. It also might help compensate for your rough morning. Don't worry, we won't try to get you drunk!" he chuckled as he stood to leave. "We're leaving at six. Hope you can make it," Chris said as he walked out of her office without waiting for a response.

"Okay, thanks. I'll let you know." Stacey stood up and walked over to her door to shut it behind him. She leaned against the door and sighed. "Okay, I have to get back to work. I'll do this later when I get a break." She sat back down at her desk and began to work on her campaign.

She worked for a few hours but kept staring at Charles's picture on her desk. She knew he probably didn't want to talk to her, but she had to speak to him. *I have to talk to him about tonight, so I'll just call him real quick.* So she picked up the phone.

"Hey, Charles. I missed you this morning."

"Yeah, I had to get to work early today." He sounded distant.

"Okay, let me get right to it. I've learned enough in our sessions to know that we should not let this linger. I was absolutely wrong last night. I took my frustrations and insecurities out on you. And you're right. I haven't done too much praying about how to go about this, and I should. Also, I'm taking your advice and going to enroll in a writing class. I already started looking up some things online." She knew she was rambling, but she didn't want to hear any rejection from Charles, so she kept going.

"I hear you, Stacey," Charles said softly. "I just thought we had gotten past this. We finally got down to the root of all this. You lost trust in me after the Kelly thing, and you still take it out on me by starting fights." He paused. "I know we're both a work in progress, but babe, you gotta give me a break."

Stacey put her head in her hands at the sound of Kelly's name. "Look, Charles, I can't promise I won't mess up again, but I am saying I'm sorry. I love you today. I know you want the best for me. Can we move on?"

"Sure we can. I missed you too this morning, and I can't wait to see you tonight." Charles's tone lightened up.

"Well, that's what I wanted to talk to you about." Stacey sat up and then leaned back in her chair. "Chris just asked me to go out with the team tonight, and you know how I don't usually like going out with them."

"Babe, you know I tell you all the time that you're in corporate America and you have to play their game sometimes. As long as you're not compromising yourself in any way, you'll be fine. You need me to meet you there so I can hold your hand?" Charles joked.

"No thanks," Stacey laughed.

"And actually, baby, you have to start showing more mercy nowadays since you're writing a book about it. The book, in and of itself, will test your authenticity."

"Charles . . ." Stacey warned.

"I know. That's how our fight started last night, babe, but you knew when you married me that I speak my mind, especially when it comes to the things of God. Look, you and I both know what happens when God asks us to do something." Charles paused.

"Yeah, the enemy starts attacking, and the very thing we're trying to testify about comes back in our face," Stacey answered.

"Right. It's like we're being challenged to put our money where our mouth is," Charles said.

"And I guess that's what this is. Mercy is going to be thrown in my face constantly now," Stacey whined.

"And plus, we can't get so saved that we shun the world. Girl, you go up in there and be the light God made you to be." Charles started singing, "This little light of mine, I'm gonna let it shine, Oh—"

"Okay, okay! Now you're playing dirty. You know you can't sing," Stacey said.

"Well, sometimes you have to break out the big guns," Charles teased.

"So does this mean we've made up?" Stacey asked.

"I think so. Tentatively," he responded.

"What does 'tentatively' mean?" There was no response and Stacey began to smile. "Oh, I see. Well, I'll see you when I get home," Stacey blushed.

"All right. I love you, girl, but I have a meeting to go to. Call me if you need a pep talk before you go out tonight," Charles said.

"Thanks, honey. I'm really sorry." Stacey turned in her chair and gently touched the frame of Charles and her.

"I know. I love you today. Bye," Charles said before he hung up.

CHAPTER 5

Stacey got up from her desk and walked out of her office. She headed to her team meeting and worked the rest of the day brainstorming in the conference room.

"Great job, guys. I think this campaign is going to be a home run. We have a few more tweaks that need to be made, and then we should be done," Stacey said, congratulating the team.

"This went really well, considering the tight deadline," her co-worker said.

"David, you're absolutely right. Thank goodness, because it didn't go so well on that Trinity campaign a few months ago," Stacey replied. She patted him on the back as she walked past him out of the conference room.

"Hey, you going tonight?" Whitney asked as Stacey passed her in the hallway.

"Um, yeah. I think I am," Stacey said reluctantly.

"What? You're coming? Are you feeling okay?" Whitney teased as she felt Stacey's forehead. "All right. Well, I'll be ready in about fifteen minutes. I'll meet you at the elevator," she said, walking away.

"Great," Stacey murmured through a half-smile.

As they made their way into the restaurant, Stacey saw her boss and co-workers sitting at the bar. Everyone had a drink, and Stacey rolled her eyes. "Whitney, I won't be here long—just so you know."

"Why? It should be fun. TJ is so funny. I know he's going to have us laughing the whole night." Whitney looked at Stacey with a huge smile on her face.

"Yes, I know he's funny, but after a few drinks everyone will be drunk and spouting nonsense. I just don't want to be around that," Stacey replied.

"You know, you sound like those stuffy, judgmental, condemning Christians everyone hates." Whitney stopped walking and grabbed Stacey's hand.

"What? No, I don't. I have every right to choose the atmosphere I want to be in. And if I don't like crazy drunks, then that's my decision to make," Stacey said with a frown.

"Whatever, Stacey. We're not religious people. We simply have a relationship with Christ. All we have to do is live our life and let our light shine, not judge people. That's not your business. What's wrong with you? You're usually a bit more . . ." Whitney paused.

"What?" Stacey said, putting her hands on her hips.

"Nicer, caring, merciful—I guess. But I didn't come here to argue. I'm going to have a good time, so let's just go over there, okay?" Whitney started walking toward the bar.

THE MERCY OF HUMANITY

Stacey took a deep breath and followed her. She sat at the bar quietly and listened to the conversations. She jumped in here and there but wasn't really participating. Her mind kept wandering to Charles, the writing class, and what Whitney had said. After everyone had a few drinks and some appetizers, Stacey spoke up. "Well, guys, I have to say good night."

"Aw, c'mon, Stacey. I haven't gotten to my new comedy routine," TJ yelled from the end of the bar.

"Oh, TJ, I know it's going to be funny, but I had some plans with my husband that I need to get to. Maybe next time," Stacey said as she stood up from the barstool. She could feel Whitney staring at her, but she didn't look back. She quickly walked out of the bar and got into her car.

As she drove home, she talked to herself. *Now, that was a waste of time. Charles and Whitney can have that. I don't need to be a light all day at work and then at the bar.* She looked in her rearview mirror. *We just live different lives, and I don't think I need to submerge myself.* Her phone rang, and she saw her sister Shirley's name on the caller ID.

"Hey, Sis!" Shirley's voice rang out as soon as Stacey answered the phone.

"Hey, Shirley. I haven't talked to you all week. You must have known I needed to talk to you," Stacey said.

"I know. It's that sisterly bond." Shirley laughed. "I was just checking in. I put the kids in bed and had some free time, so I wanted to see what's up."

"Well, I just left the bar with my co-workers," Stacey paused for effect.

"You say that as if I'm supposed to gasp or something. You need repentance?" Shirley mocked.

"No, Shirley. I just hate going to those types of things. People are getting drunk, cursing, and talking about fornication. You name it, it's there," Stacey complained.

"Okay. Are you participating in those things? Wait, don't answer that. I know the answer is no, Stacey, and so do your co-workers. They know who you are and what you stand for. Why are you so annoyed?" Shirley asked.

"Okay, I'm the older sister, so don't start trying to chastise me." Stacey said as she stopped at the railroad tracks.

"Oh, Stacey, I'm not chastising you. I'm keeping it real. We talk all the time about this type of stuff. Sometimes we have to do things and mingle with people who are not like us."

"Really? I think I know this, little sis," Stacey snapped.

"Okay, how about this? Remember when we were in Richmond at Grandma's house that one summer?"

"We went to Grandma's house lots of summers. Which one are you talking about?" Stacey asked.

"You'll remember in a minute. We were in the living room playing our own made-up game since Grandma didn't have a television," Shirley said.

"Oh, yeah. We had to make up a lot of stuff. It was so boring over there," Stacey laughed.

"Well, that day we started fighting, and you ran into the kitchen and told on me to Grandma. You told her I wasn't sharing."

"And Grandma being Grandma didn't even play into it. You know, she didn't even turn around from the sink and look at me? She just knew what had happened and started schooling me," Stacey said.

"Yes, she was famous for that. And she told you, too. I was in the living room just laughing," Shirley said.

As Stacey stopped at the next red light, she rested her head on the steering wheel and shook it back and forth in embarrassment. "She got me good that day. I can hear her voice so clear even now, Shirley. Remember how she had that thick Southern accent from Alabama?"

"Yup. Nothing like it. But my point is what she told you that day. Do you remember, Stacey?" Shirley asked.

"Yes, I do. Grandma stopped chopping her vegetables and said, 'Stacey, all I hear you preaching in that there living room is about sharing. Now, your sister asked to play with your doll last night, but you refused. That's not sharing. If you're going to preach something, you have to live it, shuga. All day, every day you have to live it. Now you go back in that living room and live it . . . '"

"Exactly. I don't want to rub anything in your face, Stacey, but didn't you tell me a few weeks ago that you were writing a book on mercy?"

"Yes."

"Well, you're going to have to do the same thing Grandma said in her kitchen all those years ago—live it out." Shirley's voice trailed off.

"Oh, my goodness. If one more person tries to tell me what I have to do because I'm writing this book, I'm going to scream!" Stacey yelled.

"Huh?" Stacey's voice was muffled. "Did you call me? I'll be right there." Her voice became clear again. "Stacey, that's Brian calling me. I gotta go. I love you."

"You always rush off the phone when it gets heated, Shirley," Stacey replied.

"You know me too well. I do love you, big sis. Call me this weekend so we can hook up. Bye."

"Bye, Shirley," Stacey said as she hung up the phone.

As Stacey drove home, she realized that the Holy Spirit was convicting her. She had been rude and merciless with Charles and her co-workers. She had been convicted before in her Christian walk, but because she had purposed to write the book, she realized she was putting herself on a pedestal. She thought that if she was called to write a book on mercy, then that meant she had somehow mastered everything on mercy. Why else would God have chosen her to be the one to write about it? She suddenly realized that she was one of the people who needed the book.

Stacey pulled into the garage and hopped out of the car. She was excited to get in and see her husband. "Charles?" Stacey called as she walked in the house.

"In the family room," he called.

"Hey, babe." Stacey walked into the room and found the lights off, a movie going, and Charles eating popcorn. "Bad

Boys II? Again?" Her hand went to her hip, and her head tilted to the side.

"Now look here, woman. Don't come in here messing up my *thang* I got going on. What do you want?" Charles paused the movie and turned toward Stacey.

"All right, man. I just wanted to say thank you for the advice. I thought about it. I've been so caught up in the things my co-workers do that I'm overlooking my role in their lives," Stacey said softly.

"Um-hmm," Charles nodded.

"Both Whitney and Shirley said basically the same thing to me tonight, and it really sank in. I had some time to think on the drive home, and I guess I do have to show a little mercy and engage them so that maybe my light will affect them somehow. I also do need to network and allow the execs to see that I'm serious about being a team player. I mean, I have to move up to partner so I can support you when you become an actor and quit your job." Stacey smiled as she leaned over to kiss Charles and then turned to leave.

"That's right! As long as you know my vision for this house, girl." Charles poked out his chest as Stacey walked away. "You're not stayin'? The movie isn't too far in." Charles opened his arms, beckoning his wife to join him.

"Naw, you got this. I've been networking all night, and I'm tired. I know you, and you know me, so I don't have to schmooze with you." Stacey started up the stairs, waving her hand goodbye.

"You gotta take care of home first. Don't mess up a happy home!" he called.

"Okay, Martin Lawrence. See, I can't take you when you start with your Bad Boy movie marathons. Good night." She laughed and went upstairs to her room.

As Stacey settled down, she tried to sleep but couldn't. "I'm not going downstairs to watch that movie with him," she whispered to herself. Her eyes came across her laptop and she thought about the book. She immediately felt fear in her stomach. Now that she realized the book was for her as well as those who would read it, she was scared. She wasn't sure where this was going to take her emotionally. There were some places in her life she didn't want to revisit, and just knowing that God had her in His sights made her nervous.

Since Stacey couldn't sleep, she picked up her journal. As she read through the pages, it took her back to a hard conversation she had with Charles when they were living in Virginia. As she read her thoughts in her journal, her conversation with Charles began to replay in her mind.

"I can't believe all of this is happening, Charles. I mean, how could they treat us like this? They're supposed to be Christians, and they're acting like this?" Stacey had cried in her husband's arms in the living room of their townhome. He held her close and rocked her quietly. "We've been serving for years, and this is the thanks we get? We helped build that church! Why would God allow them to do this?"

"Stacey, I can't believe it either, but we have to reach down and grab hold of our faith in God. God calls us to Him,

not man. *Everyone who is in our lives has the ability to hurt us. You don't expect it to come from the church, but sometimes it does. I don't know what we're going to do, but I do know that we're not making a move until God says so."* Charles kissed her forehead softly. *"We'll get through this, and I can guarantee we'll be better for it. Come on, let's pray."*

Stacey pulled away from her husband. *"I don't want to pray. I don't want to be a better Christian! I want the so-called Christians at that church to stop the lies they are spreading, reverse the decisions they have made about our ministry, and apologize for what they have done!"*

"Stacey," Charles calmly replied.

"No! God gave us the vision for that ministry, and we went forward selflessly. We gave our time and money, and now they're saying it was they who did all the work? They can't find the money we were supposed to donate to those kids, and we're no longer the ministry leaders? I'm too much in shock to pray."

Charles got on his knees and began to pray anyway. *"Lord, You know our hearts and what we're going through right now. You hear the honesty of my wife, and I ask You to heal her. Remind her of who You are and the promises You made to her and me. You called us together to this church. Please forgive those who have hurt us and please help us line up our hearts with our words. Show us the characteristics you want us to mature in, Lord, and send Your grace and mercy so that we may withstand this storm. In Jesus' name, Amen."*

As Stacey remembered her husband's prayer from that night, she realized that his words and the experience were an integral part of the destiny of her book. She began to sob uncontrollably as she realized how God had planned everything and allowed the hurt and pain in her life for His greater purpose. He actually trusted her with the pain because He knew she would use it to glorify Him. She began writing through her tears as she sat in her bed.

CHAPTER 6

Following her breakthrough of sorts, Stacey decided to move forward and signed up for a weekend writing class at the local community college. Three weeks later the semester started, and Stacey was on her way to her first class. She was a bit nervous as she entered the building. She held her registration paper in her hand as she walked down the hall looking for her room number.

"May I help you?" a kind-faced elderly woman asked.

"Um, yes. I'm looking for room 256, The Fundamentals of Literary Writing 101," Stacey said with a smile.

"You're almost there. Two doors down on your right." The lady pointed down the hallway through the crowd of college students.

"Thank you," Stacey said as she continued down the hall, then entered the room. She stood in the doorway and gazed around. Her nerves seemed to paralyze her.

"Excuse me," a voice rang out behind her.

Stacey jumped. "Oh, I'm sorry." She walked into the

classroom as the impatient student rushed by her. As she walked toward the back of the classroom, she eyed all the younger students sitting in the desks. They were laughing, texting, listening to iPods, and blatantly reminding Stacey of how old she really was. She sat down quietly at a desk in the back corner of the last row of the classroom.

As more people started filing into the classroom, her heart raced. She started to make excuses for why she shouldn't be there, trying to psych herself out. *Maybe I don't need to take the class. I think I'm getting better the more I write.*

Then the teacher, a twenty-something wearing jeans and a blazer, entered the classroom bopping to some music he was listening to on his headphones. Stacey rolled her eyes. *Okay, now this baby is going to teach me how to write? Maybe I didn't hear God too well. Maybe this is going a little too fast.*

But before she could gather her things to leave, her phone chimed. It was an e-mail from Charles.

"Babe, you got this. Don't worry. Riley and I are so proud of you. I'm honored to be married to such a beautiful and smart woman. If nothing else, remember that we're home praying on your behalf. So pay attention and stop playing with your phone in class. We're paying too much money for you to be messing around. Love, Charles."

Stacey sank down in her chair and twirled her curls with her finger. She smiled as she put the phone away and opened her notebook. *How did I get so lucky? Don't be scared, Stace. Let's go for it,* she thought.

"Good morning, my name is Stanley, and I'll be introducing you to the fundamentals of literary writing. Obviously you're here because you have a desire to write, and my job is to give you some tools to get those great ideas from your head to the paper," the teacher said as he sat on the desk in front of the classroom.

As Stanley began to teach the class, Stacey started to feel passionately about what he was saying. She ended up really enjoying herself and learning a lot about writing. She left feeling empowered and ready to really dive in to her book. She beamed as she returned home.

"How was it?" Riley asked as Stacey walked into the kitchen.

"It was great, sweetie. I learned so much, and it was just the first day!"

"That's good, Mom. What's for dinner?"

"Um, I'm not sure. You want to hear more about my class?" Stacey asked.

"Mom, really?" Riley rolled her eyes.

"Oh, I'm sorry. You probably have some texts or something to get to, right?" Stacey teased.

"Not funny, Mom. There are a lot of important things going on at school, and my friends and I have to talk." Riley put her headphones on and began texting as she walked away.

Stacey shook her head as she whispered aloud, "And she's just in middle school. Lord, have mercy."

"Are you supposed to talk to yourself? Is that what you learned in class today?" Charles asked as he walked into the room.

"Funny . . . no, I'm just talking about your daughter. She makes me talk to myself." Stacey hugged Charles.

"Well then, tell me what you did learn today," he said.

"It was awesome, Charles. I really was excited about it all. I mean, merging the writing skills with what God wants me to say is going to be challenging, but I feel like I can do it now. By the time this class is over, I know I'm going to have learned so much."

They sat at the kitchen table and talked until Riley interrupted them. "I'm so hungry. I feel like I haven't eaten all day."

Stacey and Charles looked at each other in disbelief. "Uh, okay. And the award goes to—" Stacey said as she stood and walked over to the stove to prepare dinner. She continued to talk with Charles about her class while she cooked dinner.

"Stacey, I have to say I'm pretty surprised at how much you liked the class. I know you were hesitant when we first talked about it, but it sounds like this was a really great move," Charles said as he ate his food.

"I'm surprised too. I was a bit intimidated when I walked in, but the teacher was really easygoing and made me feel comfortable."

As they finished eating, Stacey stood up and picked up her briefcase. "I'm heading upstairs to do some writing. You guys have kitchen duty."

"Write on sista, *write on!*" Charles threw his fist in the air.

Stacey paused and turned to Charles. "You really want to be a comedian, don't you?"

"Hey, you're walking in your purpose, so maybe I should pursue mine," Charles laughed.

"Uh, yeah. You do that," Stacey remarked with a frown.

She made her way upstairs and spent the rest of the night in her room reading her class notes and writing until sleep overtook her.

Six weeks flew by as she attended her class. She was learning a lot and kept moving forward with writing her book. "I think I'm almost done with this, Shirley," Stacey said as she sat with her sister in her home in downtown Chicago. "My class is over, and I can see this really coming to life."

"I'm really excited for you, Stacey. I mean, you really are pushing through this thing. I'm proud of you for sticking with it," Shirley replied.

"Sticking with it?" Stacey squinted as the fall sun streamed through the bay window of Shirley's living room.

"Yeah." Shirley provided no explanation as she stood to walk out of the room.

Following right behind her, Stacey questioned her sister, "What do you mean? That didn't sound like a compliment, so what was it?"

Shirley stopped and turned to Stacey. "Calm down, big sis. All I'm saying is that sometimes you have a tendency to start things and not finish them. I'm just proud of you for seeing this one through from beginning to end." She turned back around and headed for the stairs.

"You always find a way to throw a dig at me, huh?" Stacey crossed her arms as she watched her sister climb the stairs. "You know, Shirley, a little support goes a long way. You don't have to say everything that's on your mind."

"Shhhh! The kids are napping." Shirley loudly whispered. "I'll be right back. Just go sit in the living room."

Stacey rolled her eyes and walked back into the living room. She took some deep breaths while she waited. As she heard footsteps behind her, she began to speak, "It's just that you always seem to have something to say—like you're trying to find fault in what I do."

"Stacey, you don't like the way I speak the truth. When I have something to say, as you put it, it comes from a place of love," Shirley spoke softly as she sat on the couch. "I'm not trying to hurt you, criticize you, or judge you. Mom always tells us to hold each other accountable."

"Oh, is that your excuse?" Stacey turned around quickly, glaring at her sister.

Shirley patted the seat cushion next to her. "Sit down, sister. You and I are always on a different page, it seems. I'm trying to show you I love you, and you automatically think I'm trying to hurt you."

"What?" Stacey asked as she sat down next to her sister.

"I'm not her," Shirley said quietly.

"You're not who? Shirley, please don't speak in riddles."

"I'm not Kelly. I will never do what she did. I'm your blood sister and I love you, so please stop treating me like I'm her." Shirley placed her hands on top of Stacey's.

Stacey stared straight through her sister for a few moments before noticing Shirley's hands on top of hers. She quickly pulled away and jumped up. "I have no idea what you're talking about, and I don't have time to figure it out. I have a hair appointment, and I don't want to be late. I just stopped by to say hi since I was downtown and—"

"Stacey, c'mon." Shirley looked up at her sister.

"Kiss the kids for me, and I'll talk to you soon, okay?" Stacey scrambled to gather her bag and her coat as she walked toward the door.

"Well, I love you and am still proud of you. I can't wait to read the book." Shirley opened her arms for a hug.

Stacey leaned in for a quick hug as she left one hand on the doorknob. With her heart racing, she fought back tears as she swung the door open and rushed down the walkway to her car. She slammed her car door shut and sat for a few seconds in silence. "Oooh, that girl gets under my skin," she fumed as the tears she had been fighting back spilled over and ran down her cheeks.

As she felt the tears, she quickly began to start the car. "Oh, she's not going to get the satisfaction of seeing me cry." She put the car in drive and sped off down the street. She gripped the steering wheel as she let out a frustrated moan. "Ahhh! I can't believe she said those things to me." Stacey began to sob uncontrollably, so she pulled over to the side of the road. She buried her face in her hands and cried.

After a few moments, she sat up and looked down at her phone in the compartment under the radio. She picked it up and dialed with one hand, wiping her tears with the other.

"Hello?"

"Mom? I just left Shirley's . . ." Stacey softly spoke.

"And?" her mother replied.

"You wouldn't believe what she said to me. I mean, I just can't believe what she said."

"What did she say, Stacey?" her mother asked calmly.

"I was telling her about my book, and she made some snide comment about being proud that I was finally finishing something I started. And then she had the nerve to accuse me of treating her as if she was *Kelly!*" Stacey began to shout.

"Calm down, Stacey. I'm not Shirley, so don't yell at me," her mother said in a stern voice.

"Sorry, Mom, but she just got me all riled up."

"You girls are always going back and forth. One minute you love each other, and then the other minute, you hate each other. There's something going on there, and you all need to figure it out," her mother scolded.

"So you have nothing to say about her comments?" Stacey whined.

"Stacey, let me ask you a question. Would you consider yourself to be a person who finishes what she starts?"

Stacey got silent and then shifted in her seat. "I don't know. I mean, sometimes I am and sometimes I'm not. But that doesn't give her the right to point that out at the exact moment I'm trying to push through."

"Why not? She has a valid point, and I'm sure she's genuinely proud that you're following through with this book. You're offended, and you have to ask yourself why." Her mother's tone softened. "And as for the Kelly comment—"

"I don't even want to go there on that subject," Stacey interjected.

"You never do, child . . . you never do. But you'll have to address it someday. God calls us to forgive. And I don't know how you're going to write a book on mercy if you can't forgive your friend," her mother replied.

"Friend? She is not my friend!" Stacey began to shout and caught herself. "Look, Mom, I called to vent and I did just that, so I'm going to go now. I have to get to my hair appointment." Stacey's voice sounded drained.

"Okay. Well, I love you today, sweetheart, and so does Shirley." Her voice was sad.

"I love you too, Mama. I'll call you later this week, okay?" Stacey said as she put her car in gear and began to merge back onto the road.

"Okay, honey. Goodbye." They hung up, and Stacey made her way to the hair salon.

Stacey couldn't fully enjoy her hair appointment as she thought about Shirley's comments. Every time she thought about Kelly, her heart dropped. She wasn't ready to face that part of her life with anyone—not yet.

About a month went by, and the season began to shift from fall to winter. The house began to have a morning chill, and the sky looked like it would snow at any moment. Stacey woke up on a Saturday morning with the sun peeking through the curtains. As she reached her arms out from under the covers to stretch, she snatched them back in. "Brrrr, it's cold," she whispered as she moved close to Charles, nudging him awake.

"Mmmm-hmmmm. That's called snuggling weather," Charles mumbled from under the covers.

"Oh, really? I didn't know that," Stacey smiled.

Charles turned over to face Stacey. "Yeah, girl. When it's cold outside the covers, that means we need to stay in and . . . snuggle."

Stacey began to laugh as they embraced and kissed under the covers. The sound of knocking came from outside their room.

"Who is it!" Charles called.

"The only other person in this house," Riley called back.

"Come in, Riley." Stacey sat up in the bed. "What do you need?"

"Dad, you're supposed to be taking my friends and me up to the school. Our bus leaves at 10 a.m. for the field trip."

"Where are y'all going on a Saturday? I don't remember this one, Riley." Charles was still under the covers.

"Daddy!" Riley whined, jumping on the bed. "We're going to the power plant factory! I did tell you."

"Okay, okay. I'm getting up." Charles turned to Stacey. "It should be nice and quiet for you in here today. You should be able to get a lot of writing done while Riley and I are gone."

"Are you going on the field trip, too?" Stacey asked.

"No, I'm meeting up with the guys this afternoon at the gym. We're going to play some basketball and then head out to eat somewhere."

"Oh. Well, I'm not writing today. I have to do some things around the house. You know the holidays are coming, so I need to start to get ready." Stacey sounded excited.

"All right. Well, either way you'll have a quiet house to do whatever you wish." Charles leaned over and kissed Stacey.

"Okay. That's my cue," Riley said as she stood to leave.

"Oh, no. I have to get my kiss from you too." Charles reached out to grab Riley as she screamed and ran out of the room. He chased her down the hall, laughing.

As Stacey sat in the bed laughing, her eyes came across her laptop. "Don't worry, I'll get back to you soon. I am not going to lose focus. I will finish . . . I will finish."

CHAPTER 7

As she shuffled her way through the house, pulling out winter clothes and packing up summer clothes, she found herself too busy to write. And as the weeks went on and she continued to plan holiday activities and parties, she seemed to get busier and busier as her promise to herself seemed to dwindle.

One winter afternoon, Stacey sat at her kitchen table, talking on the phone with Charlene. "Are you ready for dinner tonight?" Stacey asked. "I know you're fixing all the trimmings."

"Girl, yes! You all are going to be stuffed when you leave here tonight. Are you going to be on time?" Charlene teased.

"Whatever. All I have to do today is start organizing my decorations for the annual Christmas party Shirley and I are hosting. Since it's at my house this year, I need to be ready," Stacey said as she sipped on some coffee.

"Oh, you and Shirley are speaking again?" Charlene said sarcastically.

"Ha, ha, ha. It's not funny, and I'm not even going to go into that right now," Stacey replied.

"Whatever. You're truly sisters, and I love it. I wish I had that," Charlene sighed.

"You do! I'm your sister. And since I'm older, I expect you to cook well for your big sis tonight, okay?" Stacey stood up as she prepared to hang up the phone.

"Are you rushing me off the phone?" Charlene asked.

"Yes! My real sister is on her way, so I need to get ready. Goodbye." Stacey laughed as she hung up the phone.

Stacey headed down into the basement to sort through her totes filled with Christmas decorations when she heard the door alarm. "Riley? Is that you?" Stacey yelled from the basement.

"Yes. The mailman left something at the door," Riley answered.

As Stacey sat in the middle of the floor going through her decorations, she looked up as she heard Riley hopping down the basement steps.

"Hey, Mom, look what came in the mail for you today." Riley handed her mom a package.

"What is this?" Stacey took the package and opened it. "Oh, it's a writing journal I ordered for my book," she said in a low voice.

"What's going on with your book?" Riley asked. "I thought I heard you say you were almost done a while ago."

"I am almost done. Our Christmas party is next Friday, and then Christmas is two weeks after that, so I'm just really busy right now. I'll get back to it later," Stacey awkwardly replied.

"Okay." Riley shrugged her shoulders. "It's your book. Do what you want."

Her blatant procrastination seemed to sweep over Riley's head, much to Stacey's relief. She laid the writing journal on the couch and continued to sort through her Christmas decorations as Riley went upstairs.

A few minutes later she heard the doorbell ring. "Riley, can you get that? It's probably Aunt Shirley."

"I got it!" Riley said.

Stacey could hear screams and laughter as Shirley's twins and Riley embraced. It was the first time Stacey was seeing Shirley after their fight a few weeks earlier. This party was a standing event, so she knew they had to put their issues aside and work together.

"Okay, I'm going downstairs with Aunt Stacey, so you all be good and play nice with Riley," Shirley said as she started down the basement steps.

Stacey stood up to greet her sister. "Hey, Shirley."

"Hey, girl!" Shirley had a huge smile on her face as she reached out to hug Stacey. "Smooches!" Shirley kissed Stacey on both her cheeks and hugged her tightly.

"You look very festive today," Stacey said, laughing as she sat back down on the floor.

"Um, yeah. Hello! I'm too excited. You know Christmas is my favorite time of the year." Shirley knelt down in front of the decorations. "Are you ready for this? I can't believe it's here already. We have to do something different this year to spice it up. I have a few new ideas I got from the Martha Stewart show this week."

Stacey laughed, "Shirley, Martha Stewart? You're always trying something new and fancy. Calm down and let's start planning."

Shirley watched Stacey pull out a few more items as she stood up and moved to the couch. "Ryan and Blake are upstairs challenging Riley to a game of Scrabble. They think because they're getting better at reading, they know every word out there. I think Riley may let them win this time. Knowing her, she'll say it's their Christmas present."

Both women threw their heads back and laughed, and Stacey nodded her head in agreement. "I can't believe they're going to be seven this year. Stacey, when did we grow up and have these kids and husbands and grown-up lives?"

"Overnight, it seems. I wish it would slow down sometimes. Riley is getting older and wiser beyond her years, and I can't keep up. Did you finish your shopping yet? We still have to figure out what we're getting for Mom and Dad." The elephant in the room seemed to disappear as Stacey chatted with her sister.

"I'm almost done. I think I found something for them, but we can talk about that after the party planning. I'm so excited about the party. I think you're going to like my ideas." Shirley beamed with excitement.

"Okay, Shirley Stewart. Do you still record yourself at home for your own show?" Stacey laughed at her younger sister.

"Laugh now, but I am going to have my own show one day. I've already written out the material for my first show, and I'm having Brian tape me after the holidays so I can send it in to *The Today Show*. They're having a contest, you know." Shirley sat up straight and flung her hair back.

"All right, Shirley. I'm not mad at you. Go after what you want. Who am I to try and stop you? But for now, can we focus on this party?" Stacey smirked as she settled down next to her sister on the couch.

"What's this, Stace?" Shirley said as she held up the writing journal Riley had delivered earlier.

Stacey rolled her eyes. "Oh, that's a writing journal I ordered. It came in the mail today."

"Oh, for your book?" Shirley asked cautiously.

"Yes, for my book," Stacey responded.

Shirley turned toward Stacey and looked her in the eye as she spoke. "Look, Stacey, I'm so sorry about what I said last time you were at my house. I know sometimes our wires get crossed, but I really was trying to let you know how proud I am of you."

"Shirley, it's okay. Let's just move on." Stacey looked down at the journal.

"No, I need you to know that I love you and support you," Shirley smiled. "I know you're going to finish this book, and it's going to be awesome. I should have known from the beginning that you would not let anything stop you."

Shirley's words began to make Stacey uncomfortable. She stood up and walked over to the boxes in the middle of the floor and began to fumble through them as a distraction. "Thank you, Shirley. I know you love and support me, which is why we can just move on. Okay?" Her voice rose.

"My sister, an author, and me, a talk show host. Mom is going to be so proud." Shirley went on.

"Yeah, she is. Here, can you go through this and see which candles you think we should use this year?" Stacey pointed to one of the boxes as she sat on the floor.

"When will I be able to read it? You know I love to read," Shirley said as she stood up from the couch.

"When I'm done." Stacey felt her words slice through the air.

"Oh, I thought you were almost done," Shirley kept pressing as she pulled her box next to Stacey and sat down on the floor.

"I am, and when the holidays are over, I'll get back to it," Stacey blurted out. She immediately wished she hadn't said that because she knew she had just opened up a door she didn't want to go through.

Shirley's head was buried in the box of candles when she suddenly looked up at Stacey. She put the candles down slowly. "Okay, I don't want to fight, but I really want you to hear me out." She paused and waited for Stacey.

"Go ahead, Shirley." Stacey let out a long sigh.

"I believe that you were ordained by God to write this book, which means that you're operating under His grace." Shirley placed her hand on Stacey's shoulder. "Stacey, if you put this off, you could miss that season of grace over your life, along with one of your greatest opportunities."

Stacey pulled away from her sister and moved to the box of figurines in the corner of the room. As she ignored Shirley's comment, she felt her heartbeat beginning to race.

"You can't give up on this one or run away from it. You've done this so many times in your life. I know you and Charles moved here mainly because of Charles's job, but you were also running away from some things back home in Virginia and putting off dealing with them the way God called you to. You have to learn this lesson so you can move on. This book may be about mercy, but there are so many other lessons in that word. If you don't walk it out, Stace, you're not going to be able to write a good book."

Stacey slammed the Mrs. Santa figurine on the coffee table. "Okay, Shirley, that's *enough!* I hear you, but not right now, okay? I have too much on my mind, and I can't do this right now. Don't bring up home, not today. You don't know everything about home, so please—" Stacey picked up the box of lights by the steps and headed up the stairs. "Let's just do what you came here for, okay?"

Shirley nodded gracefully and let her sister off the hook. They continued to plan the party and conveniently ignored the elephant that had re-entered the room.

CHAPTER 8

Later that evening after Shirley left, Stacey walked into the living room. It was a little chilly, so she turned on the gas fireplace. As she sat down on the couch, she pulled the throw off the chair and wrapped it around her shoulders. She sat in silence as she began to think of home. Her mind wandered back to the decision she and Charles made to move to Chicago.

Stacey saw herself sitting at the kitchen table back at their home in Virginia. "I think it will be a great idea, Charles. That's awesome, and I'm so proud of you."

"Uh, I didn't think it would be that easy, Stacey. You can take some time to think about it. I mean, we both have to take some time to think about it. Moving all the way to Chicago is not something you decide in one conversation." Charles frowned at his over-anxious wife. "What's going on? This isn't like you, Stacey."

Stacey stood up and walked to the refrigerator. "What do you mean, I can't support my husband? That's what I pledged to do at our wedding. Remember?" she snapped.

Charles's voice rose as he began to speak. "Don't do that, Stacey. Don't do it. I'm the head of this household, and I will not allow you to manipulate the vision of this family based on your own selfish issues." He jumped up from the table, knocking the chair to the floor.

"Excuse me?" Stacey shouted. "What do you mean, my own selfish issues? Don't get all head of household on me today when it's convenient. All I said was that I wanted to support you. If you don't want me to, then I won't. How about you move all by yourself?" As soon as the words came out of her mouth, she knew she had gone too far.

Charles took a deep breath and walked toward Stacey. "Look, this conversation just went from zero to a hundred in thirty seconds." His voice began to calm. "That should show you something is wrong. If you don't want to admit it, fine. But I'm going to be the head of this house and pray about it. I'm also going to pray about you being a bit more real with yourself and me and not hiding behind insults." He walked out of the kitchen and out the front door, slamming it behind him.

The memory of the door slamming brought her back to reality. She touched her face as she felt tears on her cheek.

"Mom? Why are you crying?" Riley asked.

"Oh, Riley, you startled me," Stacey said, looking up at her daughter. "I was just . . . um, doing some reminiscing. Sometimes I get emotional when I do that, but I'm okay."

She smiled at Riley and held out her arms, beckoning for a hug. Riley knelt down on the floor to give her a hug. Stacey kissed the top of her head and held her tight. As she hugged

Riley, she went back to her memories, feeling ashamed of how she had treated Charles that night. He was right. She was hiding behind her issues at the time and didn't want to admit it. Shirley was right. She was running away from Virginia when they moved to Chicago. Now Stacey wasn't even sure if she realized what she was doing when it all happened.

"Uh, okay, that's enough. Sheesh!" Riley squirmed out from under her mother's grip. "I just came in to let you know that I just got back from Keisha's house. I didn't need the love fest."

Stacey watched Riley roll her eyes in a teenage sort of way and sit down on the couch.

"Dad said to come tell you I was home, so we can go to Aunt Charlene's house for dinner. Are you ready to go?"

Stacey got up to turn off the fireplace. "Oh, yeah. I'm ready. Let me go freshen up. Give me ten minutes. Can you grab the potato salad out of the refrigerator please, sweetie?"

Stacey headed upstairs as she forced herself to stop thinking about the past. She was relieved she had somewhere to go where she could focus on the present and just have a good time.

As they piled into the car, Riley squealed. "Shoot! I forgot the potato salad! I'll be right back."

After Riley ran back into the house, Stacey leaned over and kissed Charles on the neck. "Awww, shucks! Don't start nothin' you can't finish, girl." Charles turned to his wife and smiled.

"That was just a thank you for being a great man. I really do appreciate you, babe." Stacey fought back tears as she swallowed hard. "I just need to have a good time tonight, okay?"

Charles placed his hand on Stacey's knee. "You're too hard on yourself sometimes, honey. I heard you and Shirley earlier today. No one is perfect, Stacey, and everyone makes mistakes. When you have people who love you, they feel entitled to share. But sometimes you have to take that information and place it on a shelf and leave it there. You may never use it, or God may confirm it. But you can't internalize everything every time someone shares something with you. Okay?"

Charles took Stacey's chin in his hand, turning her face toward his. "I love you, and as husband and wife, it's up to us to work through our mess together. Let's go and have a nice time tonight. We're probably going to play Scrabble, and I need you fired up so we can take down Tim and Charlene. Now, I love you, girl, but if you ain't right. I'm goin' to have to bench you."

Stacey snatched her chin from Charles's hand. "Charles! You are such a sucka. How are you going to bench your wife? For better or worse, right?" Stacey leaned back toward the window, eyeing him.

"Yes, but when you're at your worst, I have the power of attorney to make decisions for you—and my decision would be to bench you. It's called tough love, babe," Charles said as he started the car. After Riley returned with the potato salad, the three of them headed to Charlene's house.

They pulled up to Charlene's house, which was already decorated for Christmas. Stacey was admiring all the lights, thinking about how she wasn't quite finished with her house. "Charlene makes me sick! She's always showing off with her Christmas decorations. That's okay. She's going to be asking me for a loan to pay her electricity bill next month. Look at all those lights."

"Don't be jealous, honey. It's not becoming," Charles smirked.

"Good one, Dad," Riley chimed in from the back. "Plus, I like the reindeer and all the trees with lights on them. It looks like she has a whole bunch of Christmas trees in her front yard," Riley said as she looked out the window.

"What? Is it 'Gang Up on Mommy Day'?" Stacey said, repeating a line from a movie. They all erupted in laughter as they got out of the car.

"She had to have a company come and put all those lights on the roof of the house. I have to admit it is absolutely beautiful," Stacey said as they walked up the sidewalk to the front door.

Charlene opened the door before they could even ring the doorbell. "Hey, guys, perfect timing. The food's almost ready. Come on in."

"Mmm," Stacey said as she walked into the house with Charles and Riley. "I smell your homemade cakes, pies, and hot cider." She noticed even more elaborate decorations as they made their way to the living room.

"Well, you threatened me earlier to cook some good food, so did I have a choice?" Charlene laughed. "Have a seat, and we'll be right in."

Surveying the living room, Charles and Stacey both saw the Scrabble game at the same time.

"I'm watching you, Stacey Brighton, I'm watching you," Charles whispered as he pointed at his wife and the game and then back at his wife.

"I'll be upstairs with the twins," Riley said with a little wave.

"Oh, Tim, the kids must have left the Scrabble game out when they were playing earlier. Remind me to get on them for this," Charlene said as she and Tim walked in carrying a tray of hors d'oeuvres. "As a matter of fact, why don't I have them come down right now and clean it up?" Charlene said playfully.

"Oh no, don't bother them." Charles reached his hand across the game board, blocking Charlene. "Since it's here maybe we should exercise our brains and have a little game. I mean, what's a game between friends, right?" Charles began to gather the letters to start the game.

"Slow down, soldier. We'll get to that. We need to eat first because I don't want to rush our time together," Tim said.

"Yeah, you're right. Let's just catch up for now," Charles replied.

The two couples sat on facing love seats and talked. The ladies started with clothes and nails while the men talked about basketball and football.

"Okay," Charlene said, looking at the other three. "So when are we going to get back to our book club/Bible study again? I have a great book for us to study."

"I think right after the holidays will be great." Charles reached across the table to pick up a few hors d'oeuvres.

"Don't ruin your appetite, sir." Stacey smacked his hand.

"I think we should invite some other couples, too. We always have great conversation, and although we won't stop being each other's accountability partners, I think adding some people to the group will help expand our discussions," Tim said as he stood up.

"Going to check on the food?" Charlene asked.

"Yes, we should be ready to eat now. I'll meet you all in the dining room."

Stacey stood at the entrance of the dining room and caught her breath. "It's absolutely beautiful in here, Charlene!"

"Thanks," Charlene said. "I should help Tim with the food."

Stacey couldn't help but stare. The dining room table was set with full place settings and expensive china. The chandelier was shining as if it had been cleaned and polished just for the occasion, and a gold runner in the center of the table complimented the rich grain of the wood.

Charlene joined Tim in making relays to and from the kitchen, bringing in dish after dish, until the table began to look like a Thanksgiving feast.

"I'll go get the kids." Charles headed toward the stairs.

After the table was set and everyone was seated, they began to eat and talk about the things going on back home in Virginia. "Well, I heard that Ramone is having *another* baby with a different girl this time. I think this is his sixth baby and fifth baby's mamma," Stacey said in a judgmental tone.

"I am so glad that Charles swooped you up before you got caught up in that mess, Stacey," Tim teased.

"Oh, I clearly saved him from that girl . . . what was her name? Oh, yeah. Sarah. Trust me." Stacey shot Charles an evil look.

"Hey, don't get me in trouble, man." Charles pointed his fork at Tim. "Wait! I see what he's doing. Babe, don't listen to him. He's trying to create strife between us before we sit down to play them in Scrabble. We are united, bruh. Don't mess with us." Charles shifted his chair closer to his wife.

"Whatever. We are too good to stoop so low," Charlene said, pointing back with her fork. "Stacey, did you know that the church back home is having their conference next week? Are you all going?" she asked.

"I don't think so. Not this time. Both Charles and I have so much going on at work, so I don't think we're going to make it. Are y'all?" Stacey asked.

"I know I am. Tim may have to stay home this time." Charlene paused, staring at her husband, who quickly looked down at his plate, avoiding her gaze.

"What?" Charles immediately asked, seeing their interaction. "What's that all about?" He waved his hand back and forth between Tim and Charlene.

"That means Charlene has something to say, and Tim is unsure if she should say it," Stacey answered her husband for them. Stacey and Charlene had known each other for so long that they knew almost everything about each other, down to the way they approached conflict.

"Well, while I'm there I am actually going to stop by and see Ms. Beverly."

The room fell quiet for several seconds. In the silence Stacey could feel the rage building inside her. She took a few deep breaths before she spoke. "Why would you be going to see her?" She looked Charlene squarely in the face.

"Stacey, she's sick, and they're not sure if she's going to make it," Charlene said quietly.

"Charlene, really? Are you close to her? Why do you need to go see her?" Stacey's voice started to get louder.

"Well, I was talking to your mom, and she's really upset about it and asked if I would go see her. They say the visits help," Charlene said as she looked to Tim for help.

"So, no one else can go? You have to go?" Stacey said, crossing her arms.

"No, I don't have to go, but I want to go. Stacey, life is too short. She didn't do anything to me, or even to you, for that matter." Charlene looked her friend in the eye.

"She stood by her daughter against my family. That is what she did to me. After what they put my family through, you want to give them support? How could you? I thought we were closer than that, but I guess—"

Charles interrupted his wife. "Ladies, maybe we need to talk about this later," he said in a calm tone.

"No, we can talk about this now," Charlene said. "Stacey, I know what Kelly did was horrible, but you're also blaming her for some things that she had no control over and could not be responsible for. Plus, these things happened over fifteen years ago. When are you going to let it go?" Charlene leaned over the table to get closer to Stacey.

"No. What Kelly did was unthinkable. She had a part in everything that happened! Obviously you can't see that, so do what you want to do, Charlene. Do what you want to do." Stacey stood.

Charlene also stood, and said, "Mercy, right? That's what your book is about?"

"Okay, okay, honey. Why don't you sit down now? Let's not get out of control." Tim tugged on his wife's arm.

As she pulled away from him, she continued, "No, we are not out of control. We're right where we're supposed to be. How can your book be about mercy, which inevitably includes forgiveness and grace, yet you choose not to exhibit those things in this area of your life? Kelly is a totally different person today."

Stacey threw her hands up in the air in frustration as Charlene kept speaking. "She still struggles like we all do. I'm not saying you forgive and go back to being best friends, but for your own growth and salvation, you have to forgive this woman and let it go." Charlene leaned on the table and waited for Stacey's response.

"Charlene, I'm not asking for your advice, and I can't tell you what to do. But I can leave this house, which is what I'm doing right now!" Stacey turned to Charles. "I'm ready to go."

"Shelf." Charles coughed as he stood up. "Put it on a shelf." Stacey rolled her eyes and walked toward the door.

"You're leaving? For real, Stace?" Charlene called. "I'm your friend and you know it. I'm telling you the truth, and you know it, so don't guilt-trip me because I won't have it. You aren't perfect. No one is and, therefore, none of us is exempt from some real talk and sometimes harsh words of reality." Her voice softened as she grabbed Stacey by the shoulders. "You are my family. I'm always on your side, which is why I'm sharing with you."

"Charles, I'll be in the car!" Stacey pulled away from Charlene, got her coat from the closet, and stormed out the door.

"Come on, Riley," Charles said as he followed behind Stacey. "I'm sorry, guys. I wasn't expecting this."

"It's not your fault," Charlene said as Tim put his arm around her.

"We'll talk in a few days," Tim held out his hand to Charles. They shook hands and Charles and Riley joined Stacey in the car.

The ride home was silent. This was exactly the place she knew the book would take her. Stacey was so frustrated because she wanted to enter this very delicate area of her past under her terms, but tonight's events blew that out of the water.

As they entered the house, Riley asked, "What happened at Aunt Charlene's? Why are you guys so mad? I didn't even get to finish my dinner."

"Just some grown-up talk, Ry Ry. Don't worry about it. Go upstairs and get ready for bed," Charles said as he kissed his daughter's head and sent her to her room. "I'll make you something to eat and bring it up to you, okay?"

"All right, I guess," Riley replied.

"Stacey, we won't talk about this today, but we will talk about it later," Charles said as Stacey followed Riley upstairs.

"Oooh, Mom, you're in trouble," Riley teased.

"I think I actually am this time," Stacey said as she hugged her daughter and kissed her good night. "I love you, sweetie."

Stacey walked into her bedroom and closed the door behind her. As she scanned the room, she came across her laptop and let out a sigh. "I never thought You expected me to turn myself inside out for this book." She walked over and sat down on the corner of the bed. She began to take her clothes off and headed to the bathroom to draw a bath.

"Lord, I don't think I can do this. I really don't," she said as she sank down into the tub. As she sat in the water, she replayed the night in her mind with mixed emotions. "You're going to have to do something or say something because at this point, I don't think I'm going to make it through this book, Lord."

With no response from heaven, she finished bathing and got ready for bed. She didn't say a word as she passed Charles on the way out of the bathroom. She got into bed and turned off the lamp on her nightstand. She lay in bed and cried silently as she realized that she had some serious issues she was going to have to face real soon. She had feelings of regret for even starting the whole book process. "I was fine where I was. Why are You taking me backwards when I've come so far?" she prayed. She stared out the window until she fell asleep.

CHAPTER 9

Christmas came and went with no discussion of what happened at Charlene's. Charles avoided it, and Stacey knew she wasn't going to bring it up herself. The week after Christmas, Stacey was preparing to go to a luncheon at work to celebrate the new year.

"Whitney, are you ready to go on over to the restaurant?" Stacey asked, poking her head into Whitney's office.

"Just about ready. How about five minutes? I need to finish this e-mail," Whitney said as she typed away on the computer.

"Okay, meet me at the elevator," Stacey said as she walked back to her office. She gathered her things and made her way to the lobby.

"I'm pretty tired, so I hope this doesn't last long," Whitney said as they met at the elevator.

"I hear you. I've been going and going so much because of the holidays that I'm looking forward to this weekend and doing absolutely nothing." Stacey smiled as they stepped into the elevator.

"I'll drive this time," Whitney said when they entered the garage. The two women chatted about the holidays and their families on the way to the restaurant. They entered the restaurant and sat down at the company table, just as the vice president started his speech.

"We have had a very profitable year, and I'm looking forward to nothing but great things next year. We have a dedicated team here, and I want to congratulate you for all your hard work. Now, I believe in setting goals, not only for the company, but for ourselves individually. So, right before I share my goals for next year, why don't you take some time to talk with the person next to you about what your New Year's resolutions are."

Stacey smiled as she turned to Whitney. "Well, Whitney, what'll it be?"

Whitney tugged at her cardigan and pushed up her glasses. "Actually, I've really been thinking hard about this lately. They've been teaching a lot about self-analysis at church these past few weeks. We're always so quick to judge other people, but we don't take the time to judge ourselves."

"Oh, wow, that sounds good . . ." Stacey tried to sound excited.

"So it really hit me hard, and I'm going to work on consistently giving myself a once-over. I want to be able to be real with myself, accept my flaws but work on changing them, and not stay in the same place all year. I know it will be hard, but how can I call myself a Christian and try to witness to other people when I'm not doing what God called me to do in the first place? I mean, I can't preach to someone about love when I'm not loving, or faith when I have none, or even forgiveness if I'm holding grudges."

Whitney reached out and touched Stacey's arm. "I'm sorry. I'm just gabbing away. That's how I know I'm passionate about something. I just start gabbing all over the place. What are your resolutions, Stacey?"

Stacey immediately got uncomfortable. "Oh, I haven't put as much thought into it as you have," Stacey laughed nervously. "But I do want to be a bit more diligent in finishing what I start. I have some unfinished things on my plate, and I just want to do better and actually complete them. I need to make following through a habit." Stacey's heart was racing as she tried to get through her statement.

"That sounds great, Stacey. I also think I'm going to get you the CDs of the series at church because it's so great," Whitney responded.

"Sounds great." Stacey shoved her straw in her mouth and drank her water so she wouldn't have to say anything else. She was starting to feel bad about the last few weeks. It was as if God was replaying the same thing over and over through different people. Stacey knew she needed to slow down and do some praying. She was running away from God, and she knew it.

Stacey decided to take some time off and do some praying and thinking. With Charles back to work and Riley back to school after the holidays, she would have the house to herself. Whitney had given her the CDs from her church series, and Stacey had committed to listening to them.

On her first day home, she sat in her office. She placed the first CD in the player and began to pray.

Lord, ever since You gave me this book idea, it seems like all eyes have been on me, and every flaw I have has been pointed out. What are You doing, and what do You want from me? As I listen to this CD, please reveal Your Word and Your will for my life to me. In Jesus' name, Amen.

She opened her eyes and watched the snow fall. As she exhaled, she pushed the play button and began to listen.

As she was writing notes and listening to the CDs, the phone rang. She attempted to ignore it, but whoever it was called right back. "Uhhhhh, who could this be?" she complained as she reached for the phone. "Hello?" she answered.

"Sunshine? It's Daddy. You busy?" a warm voice said from the other end of the line.

"Daddy? Hey! I'm never too busy for you. What are you up to?" Stacey was a daddy's girl and had a great relationship with him. She looked up to him and respected the way he always walked out the godly characteristics he talked about.

"Oh, I was just thinking about my baby girl and decided to call. How are things going in the Windy City?" he asked.

"Well, I'm taking some time off to do some praying and listening. And at this very moment, I'm watching the snow fall as I wait on God. It's absolutely beautiful." Stacey smiled as she looked out the window from her chair.

"Well, that sounds great, Sunshine. It's always good to slow down and wait on God," he replied.

"What are you doing?" Stacey asked.

"I just finished talking to your Uncle Ed," he said.

"Really? How is he? I haven't seen him in a while." Stacey stood up and walked over to the window seat and sat down.

"Well, actually that is what he was talking about. He hadn't seen me in a while, and he's going through some stuff with his kids and wife and really needed my support. I told him I would pray for him, but he sounded like that wasn't enough. So I offered to come visit him, and he was thrilled."

"Wow, that was nice of you to offer, Dad. So, when are you going?" Stacey asked.

"I'm leaving next week. You know, sometimes people don't know what to ask for when they're going through things, so I'm glad I listened to the Holy Spirit when He said I should offer to go and visit him."

"Dad?" Stacey felt something stirring inside her.

"Yes, Sunshine?" he responded.

"Are you trying to tell me something?" Stacey asked.

"No, why would you say that?" he said softly.

"Dad, I know you. You like to tell me what you think I should do by telling me a story. Just come out with it," Stacey pleaded.

"Well, when you put it like that, I guess I'm saying it sure would be nice if you came home to visit, Sunshine. Mama would love your company." His soft voice contained a smile.

"Why the sudden need for me to visit her?"

"Well, you know Ms. Beverly is still sick and not getting any better. It's really taking a toll on your mother," he said.

"And did you call Shirley, too?" Stacey asked, already knowing the answer.

"No, just you," he said, offering no explanation as to why she was singled out.

"So that means this visit would really be for me?" Stacey responded.

"Baby, that is up to you and you alone. Free will is both a blessing and a curse, I guess, sweetheart," her dad said a bit firmer.

"Okay, Dad. I'll call Mom later and talk to her about it. I love you and your subtle ways," Stacey laughed. She couldn't be mad at her dad. He never pushed her. He only suggested and left it at that, so she never felt like he was intruding.

"I love you, Stacey, and I'll talk to you later. I have some things to do now," her dad said.

"Okay, Daddy. Thanks for calling. I love you today," she whispered as they said goodbye and hung up.

After Stacey hung up the phone, she began to feel nervous. She knew that her mom was probably really feeling emotional about her best friend possibly dying, but how could her mom expect Stacey to lay down her feelings after what Ms. Beverly's daughter had done to her? As she stared at the snow falling, she decided to write in her journal. She walked over to the desk and picked up her journal and a pen. She sat down on the couch and began to write.

I remember waiting in the freezing cold for Kelly. She only lived down the street, but it was so cold it felt like she lived on the other side of town. Mom wanted me to come in, but I refused until Kelly got there.

As soon as we got inside, we asked Mom for some hot chocolate, and I could hear her laughing on the phone with Ms. Beverly. They were always on the phone, just like Kelly and I were always playing together.

That was the day Kelly told me she wished she had a dad like mine. We were playing in my room like usual, and she just came out and said it. I loved her so much, and it felt like she was my sister anyway, so I said yes. Shirley was just a baby, so I couldn't play with her, and Kelly was so fun to play with. I think I almost fell down the steps because I was running so fast to get downstairs to my dad. I ran right up to him and asked him if Kelly and I could share him as a father. He was the most important thing in my life, so sharing him was a big deal to me.

Of course, Daddy being Daddy, he asked Kelly a whole bunch of questions about listening to him, treating him with respect, and loving him. She was so happy she said yes to them all. I was truly and genuinely happy that day. I never thought it would come back to bite me.

From that day on we were inseparable. When Ms. Beverly struggled and had to work overtime, Kelly spent the night. She even went on vacations with us. We finished grade school together, and even high school. We never really fought, and even if we did, it never lasted long. We did everything together, including experiencing our first kiss on the same day. We planned everything and got the boys at the same place at the same time. We were crazy.

I remember that our senior year of high school is when everything started to change. I started applying for college, and when I asked her about it, she got mad. I couldn't understand why she would be mad at me. That's when Mom told me that Kelly probably wasn't going to go to college. We had been so close, and she really was such a part of my family that I didn't realize the reality of her situation. She didn't have the things we had, and Ms. Beverly couldn't afford to send her to college. I was devastated and began to feel awkward about our differences. It was like I almost felt wrong for being more fortunate than she was.

When I left for college, we talked every day until I started to find new friends and get involved with more and more activities. Eventually, we drifted apart, especially when I started participating in summer programs and internships. I traveled all over the country, while Kelly was left at home to work and help her mother pay the bills.

The summer before my senior year, I came home to visit Dad after he had his knee surgery, and I ran into Kelly at the house. We had a huge fight. I can remember the look on her face. She looked at me with such disgust. I remember that we fought over Dad, and I accused her of not fighting hard enough to get out of her circumstances. I could see she was jealous of me, as well as my family and everything I had.

I can hear Daddy's words even now: "Hey, that's enough. Stop the fighting right now. Stacey, you will not say mean things in anger to hurt Kelly. Kelly, you will not put the fault of your current life status on Stacey. You girls are an example of real life. It may not be fair, but you both have the same access to the grace, mercy, and favor of God."

He was furious. I had never heard him raise his voice like he did that day. He sat up in the bed and said, "Both of you need to trust Him. Kelly, you may have to work harder for some of the things you want, but I can guarantee the life lessons and characteristics that you will get from that far outweigh some textbook learning in college."

He turned and looked at me. "Stacey, you need to be more graceful and humble about the many blessings you have. You have them in spite of yourself, not *because of yourself. Get it together."* He finished his *speech and pointed to the door and we both walked out.*

Stacey's tears dropped onto the pages of her journal. She closed the book slowly and cried as she thought about Kelly's life. As she thought more, she wiped her face. "I don't care what she went through in her life. It doesn't excuse what she did to me and Charles." She jumped up from the couch and went into the kitchen to start dinner.

"Wow, honey. This dinner is great. It's like Thanksgiving or something," Charles said as he rubbed his stomach.

Stacey smiled. "Well, I just wanted to show you and Riley how much I love and appreciate you. We are very fortunate and blessed."

"It seems like your day went well," Charles observed.

"Well, I just did a lot of thinking, and I talked to Daddy today. He always makes me reflect on my blessings." Stacey hugged Charles.

CHAPTER 10

The next week, Stacey went home to visit her mother as her father had "asked." The air was cold as she walked out of the airport. She saw her name on a sign and walked over to the car. "Ms. Brighton?" the driver asked.

"Yes, thank you." She got into the car as the driver put her bags into the trunk. She looked at all the familiar sights as she rode in the backseat, smiling as memories flashed through her mind from her childhood. As she pulled up, she saw her parents' blue and white colonial home. It was a cozy house which reminded her immediately of her mother's warm apple pie. She looked up and saw the attic window where she and Kelly had played so many times, and her heart skipped a beat. Stacey whispered to herself, "All right, Stacey, you're here for your mother. It's not about Kelly; it's about Mom. You can do this." She exhaled and opened her door.

Her mom was waiting at the front door as Stacey got out of the car. She was leaning on the door frame and wrapped in a wool sweater. Her hands clutched around her waist as if she was hugging herself. As Stacey got closer, she saw tears rolling down her mom's cheeks. "Mom, are you okay?" Stacey asked.

"She's gone, Stacey. Beverly's gone." Her mom's voice quivered as she told Stacey that her best friend had died. She bit her lip and shook her head before erupting into sobs. Stacey's heart sank for her mother because she knew how close they were and what they meant to each other. They were truly like sisters, and now there was only one of them left. Stacey threw her arms around her mother's neck and held her tight.

"I'm here, Mom. It'll be okay," she whispered. As they hugged, Stacey could feel her mother's heartbeat. It was racing fast, and her breathing was heavy. "Come on inside. You need to sit down and relax."

They turned slowly and went inside the house, where it was quiet and still. There was no sweet smell coming from the kitchen or music from the library. It felt sad, and Stacey knew life had forever changed. They sat down on the sofa and stared out the window into the front yard. They sat in silence for what seemed to be hours to Stacey. She didn't know what to say to her mother. She had neither experienced death this closely before or been in the position to console her mother because it had always been the other way around. She was terrified of saying the wrong thing.

Suddenly, the phone rang. "I'll get it, Mom." As she stood, there was no response from her except sniffles and the crumpling of tissues. "Hello, Randall residence, Stacey speaking."

"Hey, Sunshine, I'm glad you're there." Her dad's voice sounded shaken.

"Dad," Stacey whispered as she looked back at her mother on the couch. "Mom's having a hard time about Ms. Beverly passing. I knew it was bad, but I didn't think she would be gone so soon. When did it happen, and when are you coming home?" Her voice cracked with anxiety and uncertainty that came from deep inside.

"Calm down, Stacey," her dad said. "You're fine, and your mother will be too. I'm at your uncle's house and will be snowed in until tomorrow when I can catch the first flight home. You'll have to take care of your mother tonight."

"Tomorrow?" Her whisper got louder. She quickly turned to see if Mom had heard her. "What am I supposed to say to her?" She stared at her mother on the couch.

"Stacey? Is that your father?" her mother said as she stared out the window. "Tell him I'm okay, and I'll see him when he gets back. The funeral is next Tuesday."

"Um, okay. Did you hear that, Dad?" Stacey slumped down into the kitchen chair.

"Sunshine, you love your mother with all your heart—I know. So just love her. You don't have to be poetic. Just don't let your unresolved issues prevent you from giving your mother all that she needs right now. That would just be selfish, and that's not you. I have to go, baby. Love you." He hung up the phone before Stacey could respond.

Stacey walked over to her mother. "Mom, do you want me to make you something to eat?" There was no response.

Her mother closed her eyes, leaned her head back, and began to weep aloud. Seeing her mother cry immediately brought tears to Stacey's eyes. She knelt down on the floor, laid her head in her mother's lap, and began to cry quietly.

She knew she was crying for her mother's pain, but she couldn't help but see flashes of Kelly in her mind as she knelt there, which made her cry even harder. They cried together until they had nothing left.

"I'm tired, Stacey. I'm going to go to bed now. Can you make me some chamomile tea and bring it to my room?" Her mother softly rubbed Stacey's hair.

Stacey lifted her head and nodded. She stood up and helped her mother up from the couch. "I'll be up shortly." She watched her mother go up the stairs as she thought, *I've never seen her this way. I hope Dad gets home soon.*

Stacey made her way to the kitchen to prepare her mother's tea. She decided to call Charles while she waited for the water to boil.

"Hello?" Charles said.

"Hey, honey. I just wanted to call and check in. How's everything?" Stacey rested her head in her hand.

"Hey, babe. Everything's good here. I'm more concerned about you and your mom," Charles replied.

"Well, Ms. Beverly passed, and Mom's taking it really hard." Stacey reached for a tissue to wipe her tears.

"Wow. Well, don't worry about anything but taking care of your mother. I know she'll be okay, though. Remember the first time I met her?" Charles said.

"Yeah," Stacey said softly.

"Well, she gave me such a thorough explanation of who you and your family were, what you represented, and how I had standards to live up to that I was really scared."

"You never told me you were scared, Charles." Stacey sat up in her chair.

"Well, I couldn't. She scared me so badly that I had to pretend I had it all together. I thought that if I showed my fear she would attack me."

"Oh, Charles." Stacey cracked a smile.

"The bottom line is, I saw your mother's strength that day. She's a strong woman. And with your love and support, she'll make it through this. I'm sure of it." Charles' voice was comforting.

"Thank you, honey. I really needed that." Stacey exhaled. As the teapot whistle rang out, she continued, "I'm going to take Mom her tea. I'll call you later tonight. Thanks again."

"I love you, Stacey," Charles said before he hung up.

She prepared her mother's tea and headed upstairs to her room. "Mom, here's your tea. How are you doing?" Stacey stood at her mother's bedside.

"Thank you, sweetie. I'll be okay. I need to mourn so I can move on. It's not good to hold on to things too long, or they will affect your forward motion in life. You don't want to be held back from all that God wants for you because you are too stubborn to let go of the past. So I'll be fine soon."

Her mom took the tea from her and began to drink. After a few sips, she placed the teacup back on the saucer and looked up at Stacey. "Thank you for coming, Stacey. I really appreciate it. I think I'm going to turn in for the night." She shifted in her bed. "I'm going to finish this tea and pray that God blesses me with a full night's sleep. I mean . . . lately I haven't been sleeping. I guess I was waiting for the phone call about Beverly, and she's gone now, so I guess . . . I can rest." She took Stacey's hand and kissed her gently. "Good night, baby girl." Stacey felt a tear drop onto her hand.

"Good night, Mom. I'll be right down the hall if you need me." Stacey fought back tears as she turned and walked out of her mother's room. She rested on the door as she closed it, closed her eyes, and whispered a prayer over her mother.

"Dear Lord, keep her tonight. Give her a peaceful night's rest and begin to heal her broken heart. Amen."

She went back downstairs to watch some TV. As she stood at the top of the stairs, she noticed her bags at the front door. Everything happened so fast that she hadn't had time to take her luggage to her room. She gathered her things and headed back upstairs. She entered her bedroom and dropped everything in the middle of the floor, with her purse spilling over. She knelt down on the wooden floor to put her things back inside her bag when she noticed her manuscript for her book. She slowly reached for the papers and sat down. She started reading through the pages as if it were the first time she was seeing the words that came from her heart, pain, and experiences. She was so engrossed that she read all the way to the end of what she had written.

"How can I go on?" she whispered. She clutched the manuscript to her chest and closed her eyes.

I know, Lord. I know what's next. Forgiveness. But I just can't let it go. She betrayed my trust and hurt my family. How . . . how can I go back?

Stacey stood up and threw the manuscript on the bed.

I wish I had never started writing this book.

She looked up at the ceiling and prayed aloud. "Why would You ask me to do this? Haven't I been through enough?"

The tears began to fill her eyes, and she stopped abruptly. "No, I will not do this today. I will not let this in today."

She grabbed the manuscript, stuffed it into her purse, and left the room. She stopped by her mother's room and listened for any noises. Satisfied, she went downstairs to watch TV. As she watched show after show, she eventually fell asleep on the couch.

Night turned into morning while Stacey slept until her father walked in. "Stacey, Stacey." Her father shook her awake. "Stacey, wake up. Why are you sleeping on the couch?"

"Dad?" Stacey sat up and looked around. "Oh, I must have fallen asleep," she said, looking at the television.

"I see," he said, picking up the remote control and turning off the television.

"I'm glad you're home." Stacey stood and threw her arms around her father. He towered over her, and she felt his hands squeeze her. She smelled his cologne and smiled. It was the same cologne he had worn all her life.

"I'm really glad you're here, Sunshine," her father said as he held Stacey by the arms and looked into her eyes. "I'm going to head upstairs to check in on your mother."

"Okay. I'll make some breakfast," Stacey said as she watched her father walk up the stairs.

Stacey made breakfast and cleaned up around the house. She bent over backwards to make sure her mother was at ease. She washed clothes, cooked, cleaned, and ran errands for both her mom and dad the whole weekend. They didn't do a lot of talking, much to Stacey's relief. She didn't want to talk about the book, Ms. Beverly, or Kelly. As the weekend came to a close, she began to pack her bags to leave.

"Okay, so I'll be home at 10:35 tomorrow morning, Charles. Will you be able to pick me up, or do I need to get a car service?" Stacey sat on the bed in her room as she spoke with her husband on the phone.

"I'll pick you up," Charles said quickly. "I miss you a lot, but I'll probably have to go to work after I drop you off. Um . . . are you sure you don't want to stay until Tuesday for the funeral? Your mom is probably going to need you—"

"No," Stacey cut him off. "I need to get back. I have a lot of things to do. She's actually getting better. Shirley will be in tomorrow night, and she'll have her sisters and my dad there with her. She'll be fine. You said yourself that she's a strong woman."

"I know she is, but this is a pretty difficult situation. I just thought it would be nice if you stayed," Charles responded.

"Yeah. Well, I need to finish packing, so I'll talk to you later tonight before I go to bed. Love you," Stacey said quickly.

"You know I love you too, babe." Charles hung up.

Stacey's father walked by her room and stopped. "You're leaving?"

"Yes, tomorrow morning. I have to get back to Charles and Riley and work." Stacey smiled at her dad.

"Does your mother know?" he said as he walked into the room.

"I'm not sure. Why?" Stacey looked down at her suitcase.

"She was expecting you to be there on Tuesday. You need to let her know that's not going to happen." Her father's voice was stern as he looked at Stacey.

"Oh, okay. Sure, I'll let her know as soon as I'm done packing," she said slowly, looking up at him.

"Uh huh," her father murmured as he walked away.

Stacey suddenly felt like she was in trouble. She packed as slowly as she could, getting her thoughts together. *It's fine. I've been here for a few days now and given her my support. I will support her from afar and send my love and prayers. I'll even leave some money just in case they need something for the funeral. She'll understand.* She convinced herself.

Stacey walked down the hallway and heard her mother humming. *Oh good, she's in a good mood,* she thought. She stopped in the doorway, looked at her mother, and smiled. "Hey, Mom. You feeling better today?"

"A little, sweetie. I was about to ask you to take me to the store so I can get a few things for Tuesday. I need to bake some pies and cakes. Are you ready to do some baking with me?" She smiled. "I want to do them Monday night so they'll be fresh. Your sister should be here by then, so we can all bake together like old times." Her mom motioned to Stacey to come and sit down on the bed.

"That would be great, Mom. But I'm leaving in the morning, so maybe we can bake one of the pies tonight." Stacey tried to sound excited to keep her mom in the happy mood she seemed to be in.

"Tomorrow morning? Why?" Her mom frowned.

"I have to get back to Charles and Riley and work. I just have to take care of some things."

"Oh, I thought you were taking care of someone here. Stacey, I need you on Tuesday. I just lost my best friend I've had for over thirty years. I don't think there's anything at home that is more pressing than that." Her mother stood up and walked over to her desk.

"Well, I did come here to take care of you, Mom, but I do have other responsibilities at home. I mean, Riley has so many things going on and—"

"Oh, I'll just give Charles a call and ask him to make sure he has all that covered, and then you can stay." She began to pick up the phone on her desk to call Charles.

Stacey jumped up off the bed. "No! Mom, I don't need you to do that. Charles will always say that he has everything covered, but that doesn't mean he does. I mean, I also have things to do at work that I have to finish."

"Well, I've met your boss, and he seems like a very nice man. If I call him, then I'm sure he'll let you off the hook." Her mother stared at Stacey, waiting for a response.

"Mom! You have Dad, Shirley, your sisters, and your friends who will be here for you. You're going to be fine. Why are you pushing this?" Stacey flopped back onto the bed in frustration.

"I'm waiting for you to tell me the truth, Stacey. Stop making excuses and lying to me, and tell me and yourself the truth." Her mom put her hand on her hip as her tone started to change.

"Lying? Mom, no disrespect, but I'm too grown to feel the need to lie to you," Stacey shot back.

"Oh, really? So you're telling me that my best friend's daughter, the one you used to call your sister but eventually betrayed you, has nothing to do with it?"

"Mom! Why are you bringing up the past?"

"Because you haven't dealt with the past, and you're carrying it around with you like dead weight. Look at yourself, Stacey. You can't even support your own mother during her time of need because of your own issues that you refuse to deal with."

"I dealt with them. What more do you want from me?" Stacey screamed.

"I want you to forgive Kelly," her mother calmly stated.

The comment caught Stacey off guard. She was stunned and suddenly infuriated. "What—you want me to forgive the woman who blamed me for her misfortune, lied to me, tried to sleep with my husband, and caused me to have a miscarriage? Are you crazy? What? Next, you'll want me to be best friends with her, too?" Stacey stood up and walked toward the door.

"First of all, you need to stop blaming her for your miscarriage. Those ten minutes that you found her in your home trying to seduce Charles did not cause you to lose the baby. I spoke with your doctor when you were in the hospital, and he told me it's not possible. So your first step is to let go of your conspiracy theory."

"You know what, Mom? I can't do this right now." Stacey turned to leave.

"Oh yes, you can. And yes, you will. Sit down and listen to me, now!" Her mother grabbed her by the arm and sat her down on the bed. "Okay, I have sat by and allowed you to run away from the truth long enough. You call yourself a Christian, but you're refusing to do one of the most important things God asks you to do. He clearly states in His Word that you *must* forgive. How can you ask Him to forgive you if you won't forgive others? He didn't say, 'Forgive certain things,' Stacey. He said, 'Forgive all things.' In fact, it says you are to forgive seventy times seven. You haven't even forgiven her once."

"Were you there in the hospital? Do you remember?" Stacey stared at her mother. "Well, I do. I remember waking up and seeing the pain and emptiness in Charles's eyes. I heard his voice when he had to tell me I lost my baby." Stacey stood up and threw her hands up in the air. "I can't believe you don't remember. You were there, and you saw my pain—the pain that Kelly caused—so please don't start with the Bible clichés, Mom. I know what the Bible says, but this is not something that is forgivable." She started to cry.

"Stacey, don't you ever call God's Word a cliché. Have you lost your mind?" She turned to her desk and pulled out the Bible from her drawer. "Are you telling me that these Scriptures are just plain words on a page that we get to pick and choose when to use?"

She shook the Bible in Stacey's face. "You were hurt, but everyone deserves forgiveness. You don't have to bring her into your life again, but for yourself, you have to forgive." She paused as though trying to collect herself. "How in the world are you going to write a book about mercy when one of the key ingredients in receiving and extending mercy is forgiveness? Are you a hypocrite? You say that you love me, but you can't put down your anger for five minutes to help me? C'mon, Stacey. Ms. Beverly and I didn't do anything to you, yet you're punishing us for Kelly's actions. How mature is that?"

Her voice lowered as she sat down on the bed. "I'm sorry, Stacey, but I can't hold this in much longer. Your father and I have prayed all these years that you would see what you were doing to yourself, but you obviously needed a good old-fashioned tongue lashing." She tugged at Stacey's hand so she would sit down on the bed. "I always said that if God gave me an open door, I would tell you this. Today is that day. I don't need you to be here on Tuesday as much as you need to be here on Tuesday."

Stacey didn't say a word. She just cried and cried as her mother spoke. For the first time, she realized how much she had been keeping inside. She truly thought she had let it go, but she was starting to see that she had only pushed it down inside to fester and grow. She started to come around until she thought again about the miscarriage, and she immediately stopped crying.

"Mom, thank God you've never lost a child. But because you haven't, you have no idea what it's like. You may be right, but I'm not ready for this. Not today, and definitely not Tuesday. I love you, but I'm not going to be here."

Stacey stood up and walked out of her mother's room. She shook her head in disbelief as she made her way to her room and closed the door behind her. She lay across her bed and sobbed into her pillows.

The house was quiet for most of the day while Stacey stayed in her room. She could hear her parents roaming around the house but couldn't bear to say anything to them. Finally she heard her dad knocking at her door.

"Yes?" she said quietly.

"Are you coming down for dinner, Sunshine?"

"Yes, Daddy. I'll be right there." As she heard him walk away, she stood and looked at herself in the mirror. After a few moments, she walked to her door and opened it slowly. She listened to see where her mother was. She heard her voice downstairs, and her heart skipped a beat.

She made her way downstairs and sat down at the dining room table for dinner. The food was already set out. Her father sat at the head of the table, and her mother sat opposite of her.

"Let us pray," her father said, reaching out both his hands to Stacey and her mother.

Stacey looked across the table at her mother. Her mother looked her in the eye and reached out her hand across the table to Stacey. She gently held her parents' hands, feeling the strength and coarseness of her father's hand and the softness and gentleness of her mother's.

Her father's voice was strong and stern. "Lord, bless this food and this family, and bless those who do not have. In Jesus' name, Amen."

As they ate in silence, Stacey's father cleared his throat. "Okay. Well, this is your last night, Stacey, and we will not have your stay end with you and your mother ignoring each other. Stacey, look at me." Stacey lifted her head and looked at her father. "You know deep down inside that your mother is giving you the words of wisdom that you need to hear. What you do with them is your business. We have trained you up in the way you should go, and now all we can do is pray. So because her words are grounded in love, you need to let go of your attitude. Am I clear?"

Although Stacey was a grown woman, she was raised to honor and respect her parents. She was aware at a very young age that they spoke from love and honesty. She was always able to trace their words back to the Bible, so she knew they weren't just making up rules or spouting religious banter. They were a very honest family who always spoke to the heart of the matter and didn't get caught up in the emotions of it all. So she knew what her father was saying was true, and that her response was all emotional. They believed in addressing issues immediately and voicing their grievances to one another, not allowing things to build up and spill over at the most inopportune time. As she thought about it, she laughed to herself when she realized that she had applied that specific life lesson to every area of her life—except her past with Kelly. She began to soften as her mother spoke.

"Sweetie, it's always hard for a mother to chastise her child when she knows they're already hurting. But I'm sure as you know and have experienced with Riley, it will be worse if you don't do what you need to do and say what needs to be said. I believe that I should have shared this sooner, but I was trying to find that balance between being overbearing and allowing you to live your life as an adult. I love you, and I'm still praying for your complete healing." Her mother stood up and walked around the table to hug and kiss Stacey.

As she leaned into her mom's kiss, Stacey began to speak. "I know you all love me and want nothing but good for me. I don't like hearing the truth, and the reality is I never knew or realized what I was doing. I guess it was a coping mechanism. But now that I realize it, it's going to take me a minute to process it and deal with it. I have some soul-searching to do when I get back home."

They finished dinner with small talk, and Stacey helped her mother clean the kitchen. As they teamed up to wash and dry the dishes, their hands met as Stacey reached for a bowl in the sink. Her mother squeezed her hand, sending a chill through Stacey's body. She knew her mother was still grieving, and yet she somehow knew that she wasn't just grieving for Ms. Beverly but for Stacey as well. Stacey threw her arms around her mother, and they wept together. "I love you," Stacey whispered as she buried her head in her mother's neck.

CHAPTER 11

The next morning, Stacey made her way to the airport, fighting an internal battle of whether to leave or stay. She put her sunglasses and headphones on to block out any and everyone in her path. She just wanted to get on the plane and tune out everything.

As she sat at her gate, she watched two little girls playing by the window. They were dressed alike, and their ponytails swung around as they ran and chased each other. Stacey smiled as she watched them. She began to think about her own sister Shirley and how they used to play like that. Her thoughts quickly shifted to Riley and how she didn't have any siblings. *Is she sad that she doesn't have brothers or sisters? Why didn't we try to have more children?*

As she sat, more and more thoughts began to swirl around in her head. She began to question everything in her life, asking herself if her refusal to move on from the miscarriage had affected all of those things. Her heart started to race as she came face to face with the possibility that she had created a glass ceiling for her life that disallowed the fulfillment of certain promises that God had made to her.

"Excuse me? Are you on this flight?" a kind gentleman asked Stacey.

"Hmm? Oh yes, I am," she said.

"Well, you're about to miss it if you don't stop daydreaming," he said laughing and pointing to the line of people boarding the plane.

As she looked around, the two little girls were gone, along with almost everyone else who had been waiting at the gate. "Oh, thank you so much." She jumped up and got in line.

When she got to her seat on the plane, she sat down, gathered her pillow and blanket, and prepared to take a much-needed nap.

Lord, I promise to dig in and figure all of this out when I get home, so please just give me a great nap and don't let my neighbor talk my head off, she prayed silently.

Just as they were about to close the doors, a flustered woman jumped on the plane. With hair sticking up all over her head, she had bags everywhere and a crumpled ticket in her hand. She lifted up the ticket and squinted as she tried to read her seat number.

Stacey eyed the woman with a terrible feeling in her stomach. As she took her headphones out, she thought, *Lord? You heard me, right? Please, I need some sleep, so let her seat be somewhere else.*

The frazzled woman walked down the aisle, looking at each row for the number. She started to slow down as she reached Stacey's row.

"Oh, no! I need the window. I just can't fly without being by the window," the woman protested. She turned around to find a flight attendant. "Excuse me? Can you help me? My seat is here in the middle, and I need a window seat. I just can't do it. I'll just lose my mind!" Her arms were flailing around, and Stacey's eyes got big as she realized her prayer was not going to be answered the way she wanted.

A voice came from a few rows back on the other side of the plane. "You can have my seat, ma'am. I have a window seat, so sit here and I'll take your middle seat." Stacey jumped up on her knees to see who it was. She smiled as she saw that it was the nice gentlemen who saved her from missing her plane. She turned around and sat in her seat.

"Thank You, Jesus. I owe You one," Stacey mumbled under her breath.

The woman gladly took the offer for the window seat, and the gentleman made his way to his new seat next to Stacey. Dressed in slacks and a nice polo shirt, he was an older man with grey hair and seemed to be in great shape for his age. Stacey figured he would pull out a laptop or a book and be focused during the flight and, hopefully, not want to have a conversation. She waited for him to sit down so she could thank him lest she seem rude.

"Thanks a lot. I was looking forward to a quiet ride today," Stacey said with a smile.

"You're welcome. I fly all the time, so I don't have a preference for a particular seat. Just get me to my destination, and I'm grateful." He laughed. "By the way, I'm Christian, and you are?" he extended his hand to Stacey.

"Oh, my name is Stacey. It's nice to meet you." After they shook hands, Stacey put her headphones in her ears so she could take her nap. Christian kept looking at her with a smile as if he had more to say. Stacey smiled harder, gritting her teeth as she nervously wondered if the wrong person had sat down.

"I was just admiring you because you look so much like my daughter. I can't believe it. I mean, at least the last time I saw her, she looked like you," Christian said.

"Oh, wow! Well, they say everyone has a twin somewhere in the world." Stacey gave him one of her fake laughs. She waited a second to see if he had anything else to say. Thankfully, he turned his head, giving her the opportunity she needed to escape. She closed her eyes, turned on her music, and waited for takeoff.

The plane began its bumpy ride down the runway, followed by a pleasant lift into the air. As soon as it finished its ascent, Stacey leaned her chair back so she could really get a good nap. She sighed a breath of relief as she got comfortable and quickly fell asleep. She was in a deep sleep for about thirty minutes when she was awakened by a nudge. She opened one eye and looked at Christian.

"Oh, I'm sorry to wake you, but I hate it when I sleep through the snacks and drinks. Did you want something? The attendant is coming around again." He had a huge smile on his face.

"No thanks, Christian. I really just want to sleep. But I appreciate your asking." Stacey said in her nicest voice.

"I just can't take it. You sound like her too. I wish you could both meet to see how similar you are. I don't mean to harp on it, but I haven't seen her in a long time, and I just have been really missing her lately. Meeting you is giving me hope, I guess, that things may change."

Christian looked intently at Stacey. She could feel there was more he wanted to share and that he really wanted her to be interested, so she sat up and took the headphones out of her ears. She smiled. "I'm all ears, Christian. Tell me about her."

"Well, I actually don't know that much. You see, her mom and I knew each other in college, and we fell in love. We decided to get married, and we had a nice, small wedding with our friends. Her family wasn't too happy about that, but they lived on the other side of the country so there wasn't much they could do about it. We moved into a tiny apartment, and she got pregnant right away. We were totally surprised and scared at the same time. We didn't have a lot of money, so we were nervous about raising a child." He laughed. "I guess most people are nervous when they think about raising kids."

"I'm pretty sure you're right. I know my husband and I were," Stacey chimed in.

"Well, she had the baby and stayed home while I went to work. A few months later, I got laid off, and she had to go back to work. I really tried to be a good dad and stay at home, but it started to get to me. You see, I'm old-fashioned, Stacey. I'm the man, so I'm supposed to bring home the bacon, not my wife, so I started lashing out and—"

"Christian, you don't have to tell me everything if you don't want to. It's okay," Stacey assured him, because she could tell he was getting emotional.

"No, it's okay. It may be hard to talk about, but it helps me grow, and you never know who you're helping by sharing your testimony." He turned his body toward Stacey as he prepared to finish his story. "Well, like I said, it was hard on me, so I started hanging out with some of my friends and got caught up in drugs." He paused as if he was having a flashback to his past. After a few seconds he continued. "Well, to make a long story short, I eventually got locked up. My wife couldn't take it, and . . . she eventually left me."

"Oh, I'm so sorry," Stacey whispered.

"Me too. I spent about fifteen years in prison for what I did, but I totally changed my life while I was in there. I came to grips with who I had become and why I was there in prison. I got saved and asked God to forgive me. I made promises to Him and pleaded with Him to give me back my daughter."

"So your wife never brought her to see you?" Stacey asked as she frowned.

"No. I knew she had moved on with her life, and I accepted that. All I wanted and still want is for my daughter to forgive me and allow me into her life."

"So, have you reached out to her?"

"Yes, I saw her once. She agreed to meet me, but she only wanted to tell me that she knew about everything I had done and couldn't understand how a man could leave his wife and child like that. The bottom line was that she didn't forgive me and wanted nothing to do with me." His voice quivered as he uttered the painful words.

"Oh, Christian, I'm so sorry. Maybe she'll come around someday. You said you're saved, so you must know that you should keep on praying because God can perform a miracle," Stacey said.

"I've been praying. What confuses me is that she's a Christian too, but she can't seem to forgive me. I've changed. I know I made mistakes and I owned up to them, but I'm forgiven by God and I've forgiven myself."

"Yes," Stacey nodded in agreement.

"Now all I need is her forgiveness. My heart breaks when I hear children laughing, knowing that I missed my child growing up. It's been twenty years since I got out of prison that I've been on this journey." Tears began to fall down his face as he spoke. "But I have the faith that God will perform a miracle in my life. And seeing you today gave me a boost of hope that she will forgive me. In the meantime, I will continue to give my testimony of redemption and change to others who have made mistakes."

"Wow!" Stacey said as she waved the flight attendant away.

"Everyone deserves a second chance in God's eyes, so we should extend the same mercy to others. I mean, Stacey, how can we ask God to forgive us if we don't forgive others?"

He kept talking, but Stacey couldn't hear anything else he said. It was as if he was looking into her life. She began to think to herself, *Are You serious? How many people are You going to send my way about this? Lord, I'm not sure how much more I can take.*

She tuned back in to Christian's conversation. "Christian, I'm sorry. Can you excuse me for a second?" She felt herself about to explode, so she had to get away from him. She wasn't sure if she was angry or terrified that God kept pressing the issue of forgiveness. She rushed down the aisle to the bathroom at the back of the plane. After she pushed her way in, she slammed the door and began to cry uncontrollably.

As she cried, flashes from her life came to her mind. She went back to her life right after the miscarriage and how she suppressed all of her emotions. She saw Charles begging her to talk to him and her shutting him out. She remembered how she rushed their move to Chicago so she could get away from everything that reminded her of her lost baby and Kelly. She let out a loud cry as she thought over her life and how she had treated her husband and family. She physically felt herself breaking apart as she cried out to God.

"God, I can't do this anymore. This burden is too much to carry. I want to move on, but I don't know how. I want to be a better mother and wife, but I can't seem to let go of my baby that was stolen from me."

She let out a stifled scream.

"Aaahhhh, why did You let her take my baby? My life would be so different if she had never come into my life. Why? I gave her everything . . . everything!"

Someone knocked on the door. "Are you okay, ma'am?"

"Yes . . . yes, I'm fine!" Stacey shouted.

As she turned from the door, she saw her reflection in the mirror. She stared at herself, and as clearly as she had heard the flight attendant's voice, she heard the voice of God.

"Kelly did not take your baby. Let her go . . . let her go."

In that moment, Stacey realized that she had to stop blaming Kelly. She blamed her all these years, although she knew that she wasn't feeling well days before the miscarriage. She never even told her doctor or Charles that she hadn't been feeling well. She lied so she could keep her grudge against Kelly.

"Oh, dear *God!*" She placed her hands on the sink and lowered her head. *What have I done?* Her epiphany nearly brought her to her knees in repentance. "God, please forgive me for my unforgiveness, lying, bitterness, and judgment."

Stacey was so overwhelmed with guilt that she couldn't finish her prayer. She had prided herself on living a life free of those things she listed off, or at least constantly attempting to avoid them. And even though she was raising her child to love and forgive, she was a hypocrite. After a few moments of reflecting, she stopped crying and stood up straight. She straightened out her shirt, wiped away her tears, and patted her face with a moist paper towel. She stared into the mirror for a moment and took a deep breath before opening the bathroom door. She walked quietly back to her seat and sat down next to Christian.

"Thank you, Christian, for sharing with me. I know it was hard, but surprisingly, it was exactly what I needed. If you don't mind, I'm going back to sleep now." Stacey closed her eyes and reclined in her seat.

"Oh, you're welcome. I hope I didn't offend you. I'll let you sleep," Christian said.

"No, I . . . I'm just tired," Stacey said with her eyes closed.

She slept for the rest of the flight, until the bumps of the landing jolted her out of her sleep. She gathered up her items and said goodbye to Christian. No sooner had she turned away from him than she felt tears welling up again. Feeling as mechanical as a storefront manikin, she made her way to the baggage claim area and continued in a sort of daze until the cold breeze hit her in the face when she opened the door to leave the building. Gazing around, she saw Charles waiting and waving. She smiled and walked to the car.

"Come here, girl, and give me a hug!" Charles swept Stacey up in his arms, twirling her around and kissing her.

She forced herself to crack a smile and managed to utter, "Hey, honey. I missed you."

Charles put her down and looked at her face. He took her face in his hands and looked into her eyes. "Hey, what's going on? You've been crying. Are those tears for Ms. Beverly? Is Mom okay?"

"Mom is fine . . . disappointed in me, but fine," Stacey said. Charles opened her car door and ushered her inside, tossed her bags in the trunk, and rushed around the back of the car to get in.

"What is it, Stacey? When I talked to you yesterday, you sounded like everything was going great. What happened?" he asked as he started the car and pulled away from the curb.

"This trip wasn't for my mom. It was for me." Stacey turned in her seat to look at Charles and asked very bluntly, "Do you blame Kelly for our loss?"

"Whoa! What a heavy question." Charles sounded startled by her frank approach. Stacey stared at Charles, waiting for an answer. "Okay, um . . . no." Stacey's eyebrows rose at his response, so he quickly responded to his own statement. "I mean, what we experienced with Kelly that night was a few short minutes, and I've done enough research to realize that it wasn't enough to cause your body to do what it did. Something was going on, whether you knew it or not, but it wasn't Kelly." Charles stared at the road ahead of him, not knowing what her response would be.

"Oh," she said in a low voice. The tears began to flow down her cheeks. "Well, I never told you or my doctors, but I wasn't feeling well a few days before that. That's why I came home early. I wasn't feeling well, so I came home to rest." Stacey took a tissue out of her pocket and blew her nose as Charles responded with a stunned look on his face.

He finally broke the silence. "I . . . I knew something had to be going on, but you never wanted to talk about the baby after that, so I didn't push. Are you going to tell me what happened while you were at home with your mom this weekend?"

"Not now. I need some time," Stacey replied. Charles placed his hand on her knee, and they drove the rest of the way home in silence.

For the next three days Stacey stayed in bed, crying. She wasn't able to deal with the guilt from everything she had done over the last fifteen-plus years, all because she was unable to process her pain and move on. Charles and Riley attempted to get her out of bed, but Stacey wouldn't budge.

On the evening of the third day, Charles came into the bedroom and turned on the lights. He moved to the edge of the bed and sat down.

"Stacey? Wake up, honey. We need to talk." He nudged her and pulled back the covers a bit.

"Not now, Charles," she said.

"Yes, now. You will not lie here in this bed any longer, feeling sorry for yourself. You have a child to raise, a husband to tend to, and a job to get back to."

He pulled the covers completely off of her. "I sent Riley to your sister's for the night so we can talk without worrying about her overhearing. You're going to get up, change your clothes, and meet me downstairs for a cup of coffee." His voice was firm.

Stacey knew he wasn't going to let up, so she agreed. "Okay." She got out of bed, brushed her teeth, and changed her clothes. She smelled the aroma of coffee coming from the kitchen and started down the stairs. Charles motioned for her to come into the living room and sit down.

As she took a sip of her coffee, Charles began to pray.

"Lord, we need You here now. You said where two or three are gathered in Your name, You are there also. So be here now and be our mediator. Reveal Yourself to us like never before. Heal and transform us. In Jesus' name, Amen."

Throughout the years, whenever Charles started a conversation off with a prayer, Stacey knew he meant business. Even in her sadness she acknowledged and appreciated the God in Charles.

"All right, so start from the beginning, Stacey. What in the world happened to send you into this tailspin of attempted depression? You are not depressed, for your information. I will not let that in my house." Charles leaned in as he urged Stacey to share.

"Well, you were right. Mom was expecting me to stay for the funeral. When I told her I was leaving and wouldn't be going, she kept pushing me until everything just exploded. She called me a liar and said that I didn't want to go because I had unresolved issues with Kelly," Stacey said.

"Wow, that's harsh. Your response couldn't have been good?" Charles asked.

"No. I fought her on it, and then we got into a battle about the Scriptures and what they say about forgiveness. I called them clichés, and she lost it."

"Stacey, you know better than to demean God's Word like that to her. She probably slapped you," Charles said playfully.

"Yes, I know, Charles. And yes, she almost slapped me with the Bible." Stacey smiled. "She told me she didn't need me to come to the funeral for her, but for myself. She knew I hadn't forgiven Kelly and that it was holding me back. And then, of course, just like everyone else, she threw my book in my face. I tell you, Charles, ever since the idea of that book was given to me, it's like everyone is throwing it back at me. I'm being reminded over and over how much of a contradiction I am to mercy and the fundamental principles that it represents." Stacey started to relax a bit as she began sharing with her husband.

"It's like the book is a mirror, and it's forcing you to examine yourself," Charles added.

"Yes! And that part I don't understand. I mean, why would God give me the idea of writing a book on mercy if I'm such the opposite of mercy? What's the point?" Stacey threw her hands up in the air.

"I'm not God, but I can see that He's challenging you to become a more merciful person to help you write a better book and be more effective when it comes to changing people's lives. I mean, honey, people can smell a fake a mile away, so it's better to live it out now then have the world call you out." Charles moved closer to his wife on the couch.

"I mean, I'm a smart woman, and I can't believe I didn't see that. I also didn't realize that I was lying all these years about Kelly making me lose the baby so I could stay mad at her. I validated my unforgiveness. What I just can't handle right now are the consequences it's had on our family and my life individually. I've lied to you over and over." Stacey began to cry.

"You lied about what?" Charles questioned.

"I never told you about how I was feeling physically before the miscarriage. I also lied to you when I said we should move here because it was a great opportunity for you and your career. I just wanted to get away from everything, but I couldn't even admit it to myself. I caused arguments with you because I was fighting the truth inside myself. I— I just feel so guilty!" Stacey jumped up from the couch and walked away from Charles.

"Stacey, you're human. You messed up, but I'm not stupid. I knew most of those things already. I've been praying for your healing and for you to stop lying to yourself. I forgave Kelly a long time ago. It didn't happen overnight, but I did. I did it more for myself and my family than for her."

Charles stood up and walked over to Stacey. "I didn't want her actions to affect my future because I wouldn't let go. And now it's your turn. You have to let go and move on for yourself. You definitely won't be able to complete this book without doing that." Charles hugged Stacey from behind as she cried.

"I know . . . I know what I have to do. God told me so clearly on the airplane that I have to let her go." Stacey turned around and laid her head on Charles's chest. "And that is what I'm going to do."

"I'm proud of you, Stacey. Don't beat yourself up for missing the mark. That is what being human is all about. I'm here to intercede on your behalf, and you would do the same for me. I love you." Charles kissed the top of her head.

Stacey felt a sense of relief wash over her. Even though she knew she had a ways to go, she finally saw the light at the end of the tunnel. She had a plan of action, and she truly felt free for the first time since that painful night. She lifted her head up and asked Charles, "Have you ever thought about having more kids?"

"Yes," he said without a pause. "But I've known how guarded and protective you are about that subject, so I just prayed and decided to wait until you were ready. You needed to be a hundred percent healed before we took that next step. Riley would be ecstatic to have a little brother or sister she could boss around." They both laughed. "But that's something we can discuss later. For now, you have a plan, and you need to follow through with it—sooner rather than later. Not everyone has this opportunity to fix their mistakes, so take advantage of it."

Stacey nodded in agreement as they headed upstairs for bed. She thought about Charlene before she fell asleep. "I have to call Charlene too. I need to apologize for biting her head off when all she was doing was trying to hold me accountable."

"Sounds good, babe. You've got some work to do, so go on to sleep 'cuz you know how cranky you get when you don't have enough sleep. Are you going to work on that too? I mean, as long as you're making a list of things . . ." Charles laughed as he tried to kiss Stacey good night.

"I'm going to kiss you anyway, even though you're teasing me, because that's what Jesus would do . . . sucka," she replied.

"There's my Stacey! Welcome back!" Charles shouted.

CHAPTER 12

Stacey went back to work the next day and decided to call Charlene. Charlene didn't answer, so she left a voice mail message. "Hey, Charlene, I wanted to catch up with you sometime this weekend if possible. I'm swamped at work today since I've been out for a while, so I won't be free until tomorrow or Sunday. I hope you're available. Love ya!" After they spoke later that day, they decided to meet Saturday afternoon at Stacey's house.

Charlene knocked on Stacey's door. "Come in, it's open," Stacey called from the kitchen.

"Hello? Where are you?" Charlene peeked her head in the house.

"I'm in the kitchen."

The house smelled liked pound cake as Charlene walked back toward the kitchen. "Oh, you must be ready to apologize because I smell your 'I'm sorry' pound cake," Charlene said.

"You know me too well, girl," Stacey said as she greeted her friend with a piece of pound cake and a cup of coffee. "Here you go. Have a seat at the table."

"Well, if I must forgive you and eating your pound cake made from scratch is my plight, then I guess I can suck it up." Charlene smiled as she took her seat at the kitchen table.

Stacey grabbed her cup of coffee and sat down next to Charlene. "I'm sorry, Charlene. I know you were trying to hold me accountable, and I just wouldn't hear it. I was wrong for so many things, but I'm mostly sorry for taking your friendship and love for granted. Not everyone has someone like you in their life, and I appreciate you very much."

"I know, Stacey. Through the years we've called each other out for so many things and fussed with each other. It's no big deal," Charlene said as she stuffed a piece of pound cake in her mouth.

"I know, but this was huge. What you saw was something I had blocked out from my view. I had no idea what I was really doing and how it was affecting everyone around me. I mean, how long have I had everyone tiptoeing around this issue and praying for me?"

"Well . . ." Charlene said as she picked up her coffee.

"I should have known. But, nevertheless, I'm letting even that go since I've asked God to forgive me, and I'm actually ready to forgive Kelly."

Charlene almost choked. "What? Really? That's great, Stacey!"

"And you were right about putting Kelly in my book. I need to share at least the theme of what we went through with Kelly—if not all the details, at least the life lessons. There are so many people who could be blessed by my testimony, and I've been holding on to it for way too long. It's time to share." Stacey was getting excited about moving forward.

"So when you say you're ready to forgive Kelly, what do you mean? Are you going to have a ceremony or something?" Charlene smiled at Stacey.

"You're funny, Charlene. No, I think I actually need to call her and let her know that I've forgiven her. I don't want to prevent her from moving forward either."

"When are you going to call her?" Charlene asked.

"Well, I wanted to give her some time since she just buried her mother. But either way, will you be here when I call her? Although I'm getting better, it's still a bit overwhelming. I'm still battling my thoughts with all of this." Stacey took Charlene's hand in hers as she pleaded for her support.

"Of course, Stace! I'll do whatever you need. Just tell me when, and I'll be there."

"Okay. Well, I'll be praying about it and let you know." She squeezed Charlene's hand harder.

"All right. Well, don't wait too long because the enemy would love to sneak in and get you off this path of forgiveness and complete healing," Charlene warned.

Stacey paused for a moment. "You're right, and I'll keep that in mind."

"I can't get over the new you!" Charlene said.

"I know! I feel different. I was really defensive and made a lot of excuses, but hearing what you just said doesn't bother me. It was valid and true."

Charlene leaned in to hug her friend. "I'm proud of you, mama."

The women chatted some more before Charlene left. Feeling really good about their conversation, Stacey was even inspired to do some writing.

That evening, she sat at her desk and began to write about her experiences over the last few months. She poured out her heart and every broken piece of her that she was slowly putting back together.

Charles came into the room. "Hey, girl? You writing?"

Stacey turned around in her chair. "Yeah, I'm feeling so good about giving away my testimony. Did I ever tell you about what happened on the plane? I think through all the tears and sleeping, I left that part out." Stacey got up and walked over to the chaise lounge by the fireplace.

"No, you didn't. What happened?" Charles asked as he sat down on the bed.

"Well, this man ended up sitting next to me after some confusion, and he was really sweet. Charles, all I wanted to do was close my eyes and go to sleep because home had been just so overwhelming for me."

"And you like to sleep too, Stacey. Don't blame it all on the drama girl," Charles said, pointing his finger at her.

"You always gotta say something, huh? Are you done?" Stacey rolled her eyes.

"Yes, go ahead. I won't interrupt again," he said with a smirk on his face.

"So I did get to sleep, but the man woke me up. After realizing that he really had something to say, I let him speak. He told me that I reminded him of his daughter and how seeing me that day was giving him hope that he would see her soon."

"So she was a long-lost daughter?" Charles asked.

"Well, I asked more about it, and he told me this sad story about his wife, about him being thrown in jail, and basically how his daughter won't forgive him for leaving their family."

"Wow! So his wife had to provide for the family and be a single parent while he was in jail?" Charles asked.

"Yes. So, of course, you can see how the story leads to the daughter hating her father for abandoning her and her mother." Charles nodded in agreement. "So, as he's telling me the story, I'm feeling sad for him until I realize it's just another attempt by God to get my attention. He starts talking about forgiveness and being a Christian—blah, blah, blah."

Stacey waved her hands as she explained. "At one point, I just couldn't take it anymore, so I excused myself and went to the bathroom. Charles, I had a breakdown in the bathroom. I was crying and calling out to God, realizing for the first time what I had done by not forgiving Kelly."

"In that tiny bathroom?" Charles teased.

"Whatever. Seriously, I realized how much I had lied to myself and you and my family. It felt like my world was collapsing, and I couldn't breathe," Stacey said. She paused and began to smile.

"Umm, why are you smiling?" Charles looked confused.

"Because . . . can't you see? That was my moment! It was my moment of self-realization and brokenness. I was so broken that all I had left was moving forward and putting myself back together." Stacey stood up as she got more and more excited.

"That's powerful, Stacey. It's crazy how God keeps after us until we give in."

"I know it took a few days for it to sink in, but looking back, I realize it was a gift. All the tough conversations, tears, and confrontations took place for me to get to a point where God could really use me. They were meant to happen to get me to a place where I was so broken that He could get His message out to His people with no agenda, no pride, no self—just God." Stacey walked over to the bed and sat down next to Charles.

"You sound like a new person, babe." Charles looked intently at Stacey.

"I almost feel honored that He chose to break me down just to build me back up and impact His kingdom. One of the most poignant things that man said to me on the plane was about him sharing his testimony in the midst of his trials. He still hasn't received his forgiveness from his daughter, but he knows that God is still good and someone needs to hear what he has to say. And that someone is me, Charles."

She laid her head on his shoulder. "I'm not completely healed, but this is prime time for me to be used by God. I am fresh meat." She smiled from ear to ear.

Charles leaned in to kiss her. "I love you more today than ever. To see you excited about allowing God to use you, no matter how much it hurts, is awesome and inspiring. Go ahead and get back to your writing. I don't want to stop this flow of energy." He stood up to leave to let her work. "You want me to bring dinner up to you? It's almost done simmering."

"Yes, please. Thanks, Charles." Stacey gave him a hug and went back to her seat to begin writing. She was so inspired that she wrote until the early hours of the morning.

A few weeks went by, and Stacey kept writing and praying. She felt the Holy Spirit pushing her to call Kelly and take that next step in her healing, but she was scared—scared of rejection, arguments, more pain, and most of all, letting go of all the hurt she had felt entitled to in the past. Relieving Kelly of all her wrongdoing meant that Stacey had to lay down her right to be angry or mad. It had become sort of a comfort to her over the years, yet she was beginning to see that it was hindering her. As she continued to write her book, she began to realize that she was going to have to expose herself to the world for the imperfect, broken woman she really was. As fear started to creep in, she decided to push herself harder and continued to write.

Stacey let out a huge sigh as she sat at her desk in her room. "I'm just stuck."

"What's that?" Charles said, walking out of the bathroom.

"My book . . . I feel like I'm having writer's block or something. I've been praying over the last few days, but nothing is coming to me. It's really getting frustrating," Stacey said, getting up from the chair and plopping onto the bed. She lay across the bed with her legs dangling off the side. She buried her head in her arms and closed her eyes.

"What changed?" Charles called out to Stacey as he walked to his closet.

"What do you mean, 'what changed'?" Stacey opened her eyes and lifted her head.

Charles peeked his head out of the closet. "I'm just trying to get you to assess what's going on so maybe you can figure out what's preventing you from writing."

"Oh, well . . ." Stacey paused as she reflected.

As she was thinking, she heard Riley running up the steps, shouting, "Mom!"

"In here, sweetie." Stacey sat up on the bed and looked toward the door.

Riley stood in the doorway with an angry look on her face and her hands on her hips. "Mom, remember when I said I wanted to be in the school play this spring?"

"Yes, and remember when I said you're too young to have your hands on your hips?" Stacey raised her eyebrows as she stared at Riley.

Riley rolled her eyes and dropped her hands. "Anyway. This is serious, Mom. Brandy said that she's going to try out now, too!"

Stacey tilted her head to the side as if she didn't understand what the problem was. "Okay?"

"Well, I just told her yesterday that I wasn't sure if I was going to try out because I didn't know if I would make it, and now she goes behind my back and signs up to audition!" Riley walked over to her mom and sat on the ottoman.

"Oh, Riley. Well, let's first talk about why you weren't going to try out. If you want to be in the play, you should try out," Stacey said.

"Well, there are a lot of older kids trying out who are really good, so I don't even know if I'm going to make it." Riley shrugged.

"Oh, baby, that's exactly why you have to try out. You'll never know if you don't try. And even if you don't make it, you'll now have the experience that will help you in the future." Stacey moved closer to the edge of the bed near Riley.

"I guess . . . but why would Brandy try out only after I said I was too scared to try out?" Riley asked her mother sincerely.

"Well, maybe she thought if you were trying out she wouldn't make it because you're so good. Whatever the reason, it shouldn't prevent you from doing what you want to do and what you know you need to do." She leaned in and took Riley's hand. "In life you're going to come to several crossroads where you're going to have to fight through fear, opposition, challenges, and even pain. In the end you'll be stronger for taking that next step. You hear me, sweetie?" Stacey kissed Riley's hand.

Charles walked over to Riley. "Your mother's right, honey, more right than she knows." He winked at Stacey, kissed Riley on the head, and started to walk out the door. "I have to get to my meeting, so I'll see you two beautiful ladies later for our dinner date. I love you both today."

"Love you too, honey," Stacey said with a smile.

"Love you, Daddy," Riley mumbled. "I guess you're right, Mom. Will you help me get ready for my audition?"

"Of course, Ry Ry, whatever you need. As long as you choose to press through, I'll be right there with you." Stacey kissed Riley and hugged her tightly. "And don't be mad at Brandy. No one's perfect, honey. Maybe you should just ask her why she did that. You might be surprised at her answer."

"Okay. Thanks, Mom!" Riley jumped up and skipped out of the room.

Stacey stood up and slowly walked over to her desk. As she sat down, she let out a chuckle and looked up toward heaven. "So, I get it . . . I get it." She placed her fingers on the keys and began typing.

CHAPTER 13

Later that evening Stacey approached Charles. "Can you sit with me? I'm taking my own advice and pushing through the fear and pain. I want to call Kelly, and I need you right here beside me. I called Mom earlier and got her number."

"I thought you wanted Charlene here?" he replied.

"Yes, but I can't wait. It's like I have to do it now before I chicken out again." She shifted back and forth nervously.

Charles walked over to her at the kitchen table and sat down. "I'm right here. You can do this. You'll be ten steps ahead after this call, no matter how it goes. You are healed, you are forgiven, and you will forgive." Charles paused. "Did I just write a new song?"

"Charles. Stop playing. This is serious!" Stacey rolled her eyes and chuckled. "Okay, here we go."

Stacey picked up the phone and dialed Kelly's number. The phone rang a few times before it was answered. "Hello? This is Stacey Brighton. May I speak with Kelly?" Her heart was pounding in her chest, and she felt her breath escaping her.

"Oh . . . hello, Stacey. Um . . . this is Kelly's neighbor, Lynn," a nice voice responded.

"Well . . . hello, Lynn. Is Kelly home? I really need to speak with her."

"Stacey? I'm sorry, Kelly isn't here. She's in the hospital. She . . . she attempted to commit suicide last night, and we're not sure if she's going to make it."

Stacey heard the words through the phone, but the pounding of her heart began to block them out. As she began to lose her breath, she dropped the phone, and it fell with a crash to the floor. Her eyes filled with tears, and she let out a whimper.

Charles immediately picked up the phone. "Hello? Hello?"

"Yes, who's this?" Lynn asked.

"This is Stacey's husband. Where is Kelly?" His voice sounded nervous as he watched his wife sitting in shock.

"I'm sorry, but I told your wife that Kelly attempted to commit suicide and she's in the ICU. I really should get back to her son. I'm sorry if I upset your wife." Lynn hung up the phone.

As Charles pushed the end button, he slowly turned his head to his wife. He whispered, "Stacey . . . this isn't your—"

"Fault? Yes, yes it is. I waited too long. I waited too long because I was scared. I was too wrapped up in myself to do what I knew I was supposed to do." She let out a loud cry. "What's going to happen if she dies? I can't take that! I . . . I . . ."

Charles got on his knees in front of Stacey and looked up at her as she buried her face in her hands, weeping. "Stacey, you couldn't have known. You had no idea, and she could pull through this." He squeezed her knees as he spoke.

Stacey stood up. "And she may *not* pull through this. No, I couldn't have known, but God knew. That's why He's been pushing me all these weeks to pick up the phone." She stood up and shoved past Charles, heading for the stairs. "One more day, Lord. I just need one more day," she mocked herself. "Well, I don't have one more day! I blew it!" She ran up the stairs to her bedroom.

Charles chased after her. In the few seconds it took him to reach the bedroom, she was already throwing clothes around and pulling out a suitcase. "What are you doing?" he asked.

"I'm packing. I need to go home. I have to see her," Stacey said through her tears. She moved feverishly throughout the room, throwing anything and everything into her suitcase. As she was making a mess, she tripped over her shoes and fell to the floor. She lay there and began to cry harder.

Charles gently walked over and lay down beside her on the floor. He wrapped his arm and leg around her to comfort her. There they lay on the floor for hours, not saying a word. Eventually, Charles pulled the pillows and blanket off the bed, and they spent the night on the floor.

When Stacey awoke in the morning, she sat up, looked around the room, and saw their two suitcases on the bed. As she stood to her feet, she saw an outfit laid out for her and the suitcases packed with Charles's clothes as well as her own. She smiled and heard his voice behind her.

"We leave in an hour for the airport," he said, standing in the closet doorway. "You will get through this. I know you feel like you can't take another 'lesson,' but you can."

He walked over to Stacey. "You don't want to hear this, but God forgives you. Now you have to forgive yourself. Even after you learn this lesson, you will mess up again." He slowly turned her around and locked eyes with her. "Have mercy on yourself, Stacey."

As the tears began to roll down her face, Charles wiped them and said, "I love you. You're broken and damaged, yet I have a front row seat to the miracle God is perfecting in your life. You'll make it. Now, go get dressed so we can go. Riley is with Shirley."

Stacey rested her head on Charles's chest and hugged him before she went to take a shower. As she stood under the water, she closed her eyes, and all she saw was Kelly. The pain she felt was so intense that she physically felt it in her body. She somehow got herself dressed and downstairs, but she was in a daze.

There weren't a lot of words spoken on the trip back home. She held Charles's hand most of the way. When they arrived in Virginia, there was a car waiting to take them straight to the hospital.

"What do I say? What if she isn't awake? What do I do? I feel like I did this . . . I pushed her to do this," Stacey rambled as they rode in the car. It was the first thing she had said since they landed.

"You have to not make this about you. She just lost her mother, and who knows what else is going on," Charles said. Stacey just stared at him. "Okay, you'll say you forgive her, and you're sorry it took you so long." He turned to her and said, "That's all you can do, Stacey." She turned her head to look out the window, not responding to him.

As they entered the hospital, Stacey fought back tears. "Kelly Darling's room, please." Stacey's voice shook as she spoke to the nurse.

"Yes, room 267. Do you know where the elevators are?" she replied.

Stacey looked at her lips moving but heard nothing. Charles gently touched her arm, leading her away. "Thank you, ma'am," he said.

Stacey nervously shook her leg as they rode on the elevator. She kept blinking as she tried to keep the tears from falling. "Come on, come on," she urged the slow elevator. They entered the hallway of the ICU and saw Stacey's parents leaning against the wall. They greeted her with open arms and whispered in her ear that they loved her.

Her father addressed her first. "Stacey, by coming here, you've shown that you have matured. But Kelly made this decision, not you. You're not responsible for her actions, only yours. And so far, you're doing great."

Stacey turned to look at her husband and then back at her father. "So, Charles called you?"

"Yes, as he should have," her father replied as he reached to shake Charles's hand.

"Sweetie, I love you and believe in you. One day you'll let go of this and realize that it truly wasn't your fault." Her mother rubbed her back as she attempted to encourage Stacey.

"Can I see her? I need to speak to her. Is she awake?" Stacey looked at her parents.

They looked at each other in silence for a moment before her father replied. "She's not awake. Stacey, they're not sure if she's going to make it."

Stacey swallowed hard as if she was pushing herself to speak. "Then I need to go see her now. Mom, can you take me to her?" Her mom held out her hand and led her to Kelly's room.

While they walked, Stacey prayed silently.

Lord, I need You now. I'm begging You because I have nothing left. I truly feel responsible for this. When I see her, I want to be able to say what You want me to say. I need You. I need to hear You . . . right now.

"Go on in, Stacey. I'll wait out here for you." Her mother motioned for her to go into the room.

Stacey walked in slowly. As she looked around the room, she noticed that it was cold and quiet. When her gaze fell on the bed, she felt her heart skip a beat as she saw all of the tubes and the breathing machine. Kelly was tucked into the covers and looked lifeless. Stacey pulled a chair next to the bed and sat down. She sat quietly for a while before she began to speak.

"I called you yesterday. I finally was going to tell you that I forgive you." She shifted in her seat. "I . . . I was going to be mature and release you from my unforgiveness." She laughed. "Right, I was being mature." She lowered her head in shame. "'Mature' would have called you years ago. 'Mature' would have dealt with my miscarriage and not blamed it all on you."

She paused and looked up at Kelly before she continued. "I lied, you know. I didn't tell the doctors or Charles that I hadn't been feeling well. I just wanted it to look like it was completely your fault. I was so consumed with me that I didn't even try to understand why you would do something like that. I just couldn't see how I was supposed to forget and forgive. I guess you never really forget—you just have to let it go."

Stacey poked around in her purse, looking for a tissue as she sniffled. "I know now that God wasn't asking me to bring you back into my life and change you and heal you from all your issues. He just asked me to forgive you. But how?" she said to Kelly's unresponsive frame.

Stacey stood and turned toward the window. She stared outside at the trees and thought about her question.

She smiled when the answer came to her. "The mercy of humanity, I guess. We're human, and there's nothing we can do about that." She turned and looked at Kelly. "We're flawed, broken, mistaken, angry—and even malicious. And God has mercy on us all, and we should have mercy for each other."

At that moment, Stacey felt the presence of God in the room. She walked over to the bed, took hold of Kelly's hand, and began to pray for her.

"God, I know You're here. If it's Your will, please allow Kelly to be completely healed. Whatever she's going through in her life that is blinding her to Your love and peace, remove it in the name of Jesus." Stacey began to cry aloud. "Let her know that I forgive her with all my heart, and I'm sorry. Thank You, Jesus, for Your redemption and restoration. I am healed, I am delivered, and I am restored."

She bent over and placed Kelly's hand on her cheek.

"I have done wrong and did not handle this situation as You called me to, but right now, in the midst of Your holy and awesome presence I ask for Your forgiveness. Please, God, mold me and shape me. Right now I'm nothing but a broken vessel, and I need You to make me over . . . make me over . . . make me over."

Stacey repeated that phrase as she cried and kissed Kelly's hand. In the midst of her tears she felt released and healed. She knew that whatever happened, she had done what she came to do.

Stacey sat in the room for over an hour talking to Kelly. She went through the many memories they shared and laughed at the crazy things they had done growing up. She kept talking, all the while hoping Kelly would wake up. She came to the end of her memories and felt desperation rising up in her as Kelly lay nearly lifeless on the bed.

"Why did you do this to yourself?" she whispered. "What about your son? What will he do without you? Kelly, please wake up . . . please wake up."

Having nothing else to say, Stacey stood to leave. Then she heard God as clear as ever before.

"It is done, and you are healed. Let it go and move forward. Don't look back, no matter what happens."

Stacey had heard the voice of the Lord before, but it was as if He was in the room with her that day. She was both scared and joyous at the same time.

"I'm going out to talk to Mom and Dad. I'll come visit with you some more later." As she left the room, she was overwhelmed with peace. She walked into the waiting room to join her family. Charles nodded at Stacey, and she nodded back.

"Are you okay, Stacey?" her mom asked.

"Yes, actually I am. I said what I had to say, and I know she heard me." Stacey sat down in the chair next to her mother. "Mom, what happened?"

Her mom placed her hand on Stacey's knee. "Stacey, Kelly has been fighting a battle ever since she was a little girl. She has been in and out of depression, even to the point of being on medication."

"I never knew that. Why didn't you tell me?" Stacey asked.

"Well, by the time I found out, it was after . . ." Her mom paused, trying to find the right words. "It was at a point in time when Kelly was not a subject you wanted to talk about, Stacey." Her mom looked back at her husband for reassurance.

"She's tried this before, but never to this extent," her father said as he stood in the doorway.

"What? When?" Stacey was shocked.

Her father moved in closer to Stacey as he spoke. "Well, like your mother said, Ms. Beverly didn't fill us in until after you all had your issue, but Kelly actually was troubled as a young woman. She attempted suicide four times—after you left for college, when she found out you were pregnant, shortly after your miscarriage, and now. Kelly was so consumed with jealousy and self-pity that any major victory or trauma in your life caused her to go off the rails."

Stacey turned to her father. "I remember that day Kelly and I were fighting, and you told me to humble myself and appreciate my blessings. I guess I missed it. I get it now, though. I wish I had learned it sooner."

As she looked back at her mother, Stacey asked her, "Well, what happened now to provoke her?"

"She lost her job, she was having trouble with William's father, and she wasn't dealing with Beverly's death well. She wasn't able to process that her mother wasn't there anymore," Stacey's mother said.

Her father walked over to her mother and placed his hand on her shoulder.

She continued. "She came to me, and I was trying to help her, but it didn't work. She was used to doing things like this to herself, and I don't think she thought it would end up like this . . ."

No one seemed to have the courage or words to finish her mother's sentence. Instead, they sat in the waiting room, quietly praying and hoping for a change in Kelly's situation. Later that afternoon, they left to get dinner. After they returned, Stacey saw the doctor standing in the hallway talking to Kelly's family. From the look on the doctor's face, Stacey knew it wasn't good news.

She approached the family, inching close enough to hear the doctor say, "There's nothing else we can do for her. I'm sorry. If you give your consent, we'll take her off the ventilator, and it won't be long after that. Again, I'm so sorry."

Stacey watched them as they all began to cry and hug each other. She couldn't hold back the tears, so she turned to Charles, and he took her in his arms. She squeezed him tightly and whispered, "I am so blessed, and I don't know why."

"You don't need to know why. Just be thankful." Charles's words were warm and meaningful.

As Kelly's family went in to say their goodbyes, Charles and Stacey watched quietly from the waiting room. Stacey's mother and father attempted to console Kelly's family as they processed the doctor's devastating news. As time passed, Stacey rested her head on Charles' shoulder until she saw the family pouring out into the hallway. She sat up and saw her mother walking toward her.

"It's time," she said softly as she held out her hand, beckoning Stacey.

Both Stacey and Charles stood and walked toward the door. She grabbed her mother's hand while holding on tight to Charles with the other as they walked past Kelly's family.

Stacey's father was standing by Kelly's bedside as they entered the room. Rubbing Kelly's head, he said, "I promised

I would be your daddy, and I've never regretted that. I will always love you. Be at peace . . . goodbye."

"Goodbye, sweetie. I'll never forget your smile." Stacey's mom got choked up and turned to leave the room.

Stacey's mind was flooded with more memories from her childhood. She could even hear Kelly's laugh. She walked to the bed, leaned over, and kissed Kelly's cheek. "I love you, sister, always and forever." She laid her head on Kelly's chest and hugged her. She held on so long that Charles had to pull her off so the doctors could come in and remove the ventilator.

Stacey left the room and didn't look back. She had so many feelings swirling around inside of her that she couldn't catch her breath. Charles squeezed her hand and whispered, "You're okay. You'll be fine, and we'll get through this."

She nodded her head in agreement, sending more tears streaming down her face. They left the hospital and went home with her parents. As they entered the house, everyone was quiet. They each found their own spot and sat still as they processed Kelly's death. Stacey sat on the floor in her bedroom, going through old pictures. It seemed that Kelly was in almost all of her pictures up through high school. She really had been a huge part of Stacey's life and who she had become. Both the good and the bad had helped cultivate Stacey into the woman she found herself to be.

As she pored over the pictures, her father entered her room. "Sunshine?"

Stacey looked up at her father as a tear fell down her cheek. "Hey, Daddy," she smiled. "I was just looking at some old pictures of Kelly and me."

"Oh, I'm sure there are a lot of good memories in those pictures." He walked over to Stacey and sat on the bed as he looked over her shoulder at the pictures. "I remember that one! You both dressed up in your mother's clothes and jewelry, put on her makeup, and then asked me to take your picture." Her father laughed.

"Yeah, that was Kelly's idea. Mom was so mad that we messed up her makeup and went through her jewelry box. But once she saw how cute we were, she lightened up." Stacey wiped her tears with her hand.

"Kelly really got you guys out of that one." His voice suddenly rose with excitement. "She was so good at telling a story that she made your mother feel sorry for you two that you were stuck in the house all day with nothing to do. Instead of taking the easy way out, you and Kelly used your imagination and found something creative to do."

Stacey began to laugh as she said, "Yes, I forgot about that. She was good. I could always count on her to think quickly on her feet to get us out of trouble."

An awkward silence fell over the room as Stacey and her dad came back to reality. "Stacey, I've prided myself on giving you girls the necessary tools to make your own decisions in life. I don't ever tell you what to do . . . but today I will." Her father's voice was shaky.

Stacey turned around and faced her father. "What is it, Dad?"

"Baby girl, you have to move on from this. You've thanked God for your opportunity to say goodbye to Kelly. But you also have to say goodbye to the hurt, anger, resentment, guilt, and any other emotion you've been feeling over the last decade. You're hindering your growth as well as your family's. I've been watching you go through life since the miscarriage, blaming Kelly for all your hurt, and you just can't do it anymore. You're breaking my heart, Stacey." Her father began to cry.

Stacey's heart began to race as she heard her father's last few words and saw his tears. She had never imagined the pain she had been inflicting on him. She jumped up from the floor and sat on the bed next to him, throwing her arms around his neck.

"Oh, please don't cry, Daddy. I am so sorry. I had no idea. I promise you that I'm moving forward." She let go of his neck and looked in his eyes. "Today was my breaking point. I . . . I have never felt God so close to me as I did in that hospital room. He was there, and His presence allowed me to let go and forgive and get a peace that I've been missing for so long. I was healed today, Daddy." Stacey sobbed into her father's shoulder.

Her father put his arm around her and held her tight. He kissed her hair and rubbed her arm. "Then my prayers have been answered, Sunshine. I love you today."

"I love you too," she said, lifting her head off his shoulder. "Please forgive me for my stubbornness. I had started to feed on the pain and bitterness and my loss, feeling like I needed it to survive. I know that was wrong, and after today, there's no turning back." She kissed his cheek and smiled.

"That's my girl." He cleared his throat. "I have some errands to run, so will you take care of your mother?" he asked her as he stood up.

"Sure. I'll be here as long as she needs me. I won't let you or her down this time."

Stacey and Charles stayed in Virginia until the funeral the next weekend. As Stacey got dressed for the service, she looked in the mirror at herself. "This is it. The final goodbye. You can do this, Stacey."

"Talking to yourself?" Charles teased as he stood in the doorway.

"Yes, actually I am." She smiled. "Just a little pep talk before we go." She turned around and walked toward him. When she got to the door, she slid her hands around his waist and lay her head on his chest.

"Well, I think your pep talk sounded great, so I concur. Ready to go?" Charles asked.

She lifted her head and said, "Yes."

Alone together in the car as they drove down the street to the church, Stacey stared out the window. She let out a slow, long breath as she began to speak. "Spring will be here soon. Kelly loved spring. She said that when she got married, she wanted to have a spring wedding."

Charles gently placed his hand on her thigh as he drove in silence.

"I'm going to finish my book for Kelly," Stacey said. She turned to look at Charles. "I have to finish it and share my testimony."

"I know you will, Stace . . . I know you will," Charles said patting her knee.

The ride from her parents' home to the church wasn't far, but that day it felt like forever. They finally arrived at the church, and Stacey immediately felt butterflies in her stomach.

They entered the small church and sat down in the pew. The casket was in the front, surrounded by flowers. As they waited for the service to start, Stacey looked around at the different people. She was surprised at how many people were there. "Are all of these people her family?" Stacey asked her mother.

"Yes. They weren't around when you all were young, but she has family from all over the country. She had reached out to her father's side of the family as she got older, and a lot of them are here," her mother replied.

"Wow, I had no idea . . ."

"You are letting it go right, Stacey? Leave the past in the past," her mother warned.

Stacey shifted in her seat and looked around some more. A man who had just entered the church alone caught her eye. He stopped at the back pew and surveyed the sanctuary. As he looked at Stacey, she quickly turned her head to avoid eye contact. She whispered to her mother, "Who's that man back there?"

Her mother frowned at Stacey and then turned her head to see. By that time, the man had begun walking down the aisle and was just passing their pew. Her mother gasped for air. "Oh, dear Lord! Is that . . . is that Curtis?" she said, tapping her husband.

"Who's Curtis?" Stacey asked.

"Kelly's father," her dad said.

"What? I didn't know he was in the picture," Stacey said.

"Shhh!" her mother protested. "He's not in the picture. Someone must have gotten word to him."

Stacey looked at Charles with a shocked expression on her face. Charles shrugged his shoulders and said nothing. Stacey leaned back in the pew and watched Kelly's dad as he approached the casket. As he stood there solemnly, Stacey saw his shoulders begin to shake, obviously overcome by emotion. She looked up at the ceiling and grabbed Charles's hand.

The sanctuary doors were closed by the ushers, indicating the service was about to begin. Kelly's father took his handkerchief out of his pocket and wiped his eyes as he walked to his seat. The standard songs, statements, and words flowed forth as the funeral went on. Stacey never let go of Charles's hand as she listened to the tears and faint cries from the pews. She said a silent prayer.

Lord, I thank You for the opportunity to say goodbye to Kelly. I thank You for the opportunity to move forward in my life, leaving all of my pain and hurt and bitterness behind. Bless Kelly's family in their time of loss. Amen.

It took everything in her not to get up and run out of the church.

After the funeral service was over, Stacey stood and turned to Charles. "Will you go with me?" She took his hand and walked out of the pew and headed to the front of the church. She waited in line to say her final goodbyes. A heavyset woman stood at the front of the church singing. Stacey watched her breathe in and out as the notes rang out through the small church.

"Stacey?" Charles pulled her forward.

Stacey slowly walked to the casket and whispered, "Goodbye, Kelly. I will always love you." She gently touched the casket before she turned to leave.

They walked out of the church and stood on the steps as Kelly's family got in the limousines. "That was beautiful," Stacey's mother said.

"Yes, Mom. It was." Stacey frowned. "I need my sunglasses."

"You all are going to the airport, right?" her dad asked.

"Yes, our flight leaves shortly. Thanks for everything, Daddy." Stacey stood on her tip-toes to give her father a hug.

"Charles, it's always good to see you." Her dad shook Charles's hand.

"Sir, I look forward to seeing you all again on lighter terms. In the meantime, I will make sure to take care of your daughter."

"Oh, we know you will." Her mother leaned in to kiss Charles on the cheek. They hugged and said goodbye as Stacey and Charles got into the car to head to the airport.

CHAPTER 14

After they were on the plane and in their assigned seats, Stacey took out her journal and began to write. The words poured out onto the page. The writer's block she had was gone. There was nothing holding her back from free, vulnerable, and authentic words on mercy and all the other character traits that accompanied it. She had been washed in grace and forgiveness. She had succumbed to humility and patience. The last seven months had been life changing for Stacey, and she was ready to share it all with anyone who would listen.

When they arrived home, Stacey was more determined than ever to finish her book. She knew she had to fulfill her purpose. She acknowledged that she was gifted with life, favor, and many blessings. Therefore, she had to do her part in expanding the kingdom of God. Kelly never reached her potential nor did she fulfill her purpose. Stacey was going to make sure she did because she had no excuse and every opportunity to do so.

She spent the next two months finishing the book and searching for an editor. She had found a renewed energy for life that she hadn't experienced before. She promised herself that she would do exactly what God told her to do that day in the hospital and move forward. She believed that included expanding her family.

On a lunch date with Charles, Stacey decided to bring up the idea of having another baby. "So, I've been thinking lately, Charles."

"Oh, Lord. What, babe? What? You runnin' for Congress?" Charles teased.

"What? Why would I do that?" Stacey squinted her eyes at Charles.

"I mean, you're so on fire for life, and changing and affecting people, I just thought the next step was Congress," Charles laughed.

"Whatever. Don't rain on my joy and fire. I know I've been really excited since we left Virginia a few months ago, but I don't know if I could ever fully express my experience in that hospital room with Kelly. God was there, Charles. I felt His presence as I was letting go of the past and forgiving Kelly. And before I walked out of the room, He spoke to me as clearly as I'm speaking to you now."

"I know, babe. I know you've changed," Charles responded.

"But do you know that He told me I was healed and delivered and that I should not look back, but to move forward? I mean, to have the creator of the universe speak to you and declare that in your life is mind-boggling. I can't help but be forever changed. I have a new passion for life and believe I should share that with others."

Stacey paused for a moment. She raised her eyebrows and looked Charles squarely in the face. "In fact, I was thinking of expanding God's kingdom and the Brighton name at the same time," Stacey insinuated with a smile.

"Huh?" Charles stopped to think. "A baby?" Stacey nodded yes. "Waiter, waiter! Check, please. We gotta go!" Charles jumped up, trying to get the waiter's attention.

"Charles, sit down." Stacey grabbed his arm.

"What? I'm ready to go do this thang. I've been waiting for this day for years now, and I can't wait to have another baby with you. And you know, Riley will be so excited!" Charles looked down at Stacey and held her face in his hands. He slowly and passionately kissed her, sending a flutter through Stacey's body.

As their lips parted, Stacey jumped up. "Waiter, waiter! Check, please. We gotta go!" They both laughed as they embraced and kissed. They paid for lunch and went straight home instead of going back to work.

As they focused on trying to have a new baby, Stacey continued to work on finishing her book. Winter had turned to spring and now summer. She wanted to be finished soon so she could prove to herself that she could follow through with something and had matured through the whole process. As she neared the end of her writing, she gave the manuscript to Charles, Shirley, and Charlene. She asked them to take some time to read it and come together to share their notes. They gathered at Shirley's house one summer evening to go over what they thought of the book.

"Now, I need for you to be truthful. If I am going to publish this book for the world to read, then I need for it to be good. Don't try and protect my feelings," Stacey instructed the group.

"Well, before I can say anything, I need my glasses," Charles said, feeling around in his pockets.

"You don't wear glasses, Charles," Stacey sniped.

"Well, when you started writing, you had glasses, so I'm just following suit," Charles said with a smile.

"Ha, ha, funny. That's true, but you are not as corny as I am, so . . ." Stacey laughed.

"Well, you're right . . . so no glasses," Charles said. Everyone at the table erupted in laughter.

"Okay. Now that the ice is broken thanks to Charles, let me hear what you guys think," Stacey pleaded.

"I really love it, Stacey," Shirley immediately commented. "I like that it's so transparent. I mean, of course I know you, and I can read more into certain things than a stranger, but I think you did a good job of putting yourself in the book."

"Yes, that's exactly what I was going to say," Charlene jumped in. "There are a lot of self-help books out there, and you really don't want someone telling you what to do as much as you want them to share their experiences with you. That's what you did, Stacey."

"I think we can take that a step further and say that your real-life experiences allowed you to break down the DNA of mercy further than most." Charles turned serious. "You touch on so many facets of mercy because of what you went through and realized about yourself."

The three of them continued to share their thoughts and critiques on the book. Stacey was so excited to hear what they had to say and receive their points of view.

"I really appreciate your love and support, guys. I received the edits from my editor, but your feedback has more depth because of our relationships. I'm going to go back and make some changes and send it back one more time. I think after that, I'll be done," Stacey said with excitement in her voice.

They sat around the table and talked some more before they ventured into the kitchen for dinner with the rest of the family. Stacey took inventory of it all. On the verge of completing a monumental challenge in her life, here she was, surrounded by her family and friends, and she felt overwhelmed with love and thanksgiving and appreciation.

God, You are so great. Please don't let me take You for granted. I need Your love and grace, and especially Your favor and mercy. Without it none of this is possible. I will share your message so the Kellys of the world won't give up, she prayed silently.

On the car ride home Stacey asked, "Can you stop at the drugstore?"

"Why do you need to go right now? It will take us out of our way, and I was going to watch the game. You know it's the playoffs, right?"

"Um . . . no, it can't wait . . ." She raised her eyebrows as she looked at Charles.

He looked at her and then down at her stomach. "Oh, for that?" he asked.

"Yes, for that. So, can we stop?" Stacey smiled back at him.

"Yes, definitely." Charles drove quickly to the drugstore.

After they got home, they went upstairs into their bedroom so Stacey could take the pregnancy test. As they waited for the result, they sat nervously on the edge of the bed. All of a sudden Riley came into the room and looked at them strangely.

"What are you all doing?" Riley asked.

"What? Huh? Nothing, honey. Why?" Charles said excitedly.

"Because you look like you're sitting in time-out. Mom? What are you doing?" Riley pressed.

"Oh! Well, I'm about to go to the bathroom. I have to really go." Stacey got up, holding her stomach as she headed to the bathroom.

"Okay. TMI, Mom. You guys are weird," she said as she left the room.

As soon as Charles heard Riley's bedroom door close, he jumped up and ran into the bathroom. "What does it say?"

"I didn't look. I want us to look at the same time," Stacey said with her eyes closed.

"Well, open your eyes. I'm here." Charles nudged her.

Stacey opened her eyes as she reached for the test. They both looked down at the stick to look for the well-known plus sign. "Whooooh-hoooooo!!!!! Who's the man? Huh, girl? Who is it?" Charles hooted as he hugged Stacey and kissed her over and over again.

"You are, baby, you are!" Stacey giggled. They danced around the bathroom, shouting and screaming.

"My mom's going to have a fit!" Stacey said as she looked at herself in the mirror.

"You're already glowing. I can't wait to rub your tummy." Charles stood behind her, rubbing her flat stomach.

Stacey spun around. "When are we going to tell Riley?"

"Let's give it some time . . . go to the doctor, and maybe get a sonogram," Charles hesitated.

"Yeah, you're right . . . Daddy!" Stacey grinned. Stacey was overwhelmed with excitement and couldn't sleep later that night as she lay in the bed next to Charles. She pulled the covers back slowly and crept out of the bed while Charles slept. She went downstairs to the office to call her mother.

"Hello?" Her mother answered the phone, sounding asleep.

"Mom?" Stacey whispered.

"Stacey? Is everything okay, honey?" Her mother sounded concerned.

"Yes, don't worry. I just couldn't sleep, and I wanted to call you."

"Oh, and it couldn't wait until the morning?" her mother asked.

"No. Mom?"

"Yes, shuga?"

"I'm pregnant!" she shouted. As Stacey realized that she had screamed, she turned around, and then looked out the door and up the stairs to see if anyone was stirring.

"What? Baby! Another grandchild?" her mother screamed back.

"What's going on, Sylvia?" Stacey heard her father ask.

"Go back to sleep, George." Her mom went back to whispering. "Stacey, I'm so excited for you. I'm ready for another grandbaby, and I know Riley is ready for a brother or sister."

"I know, Mom! I'm so excited that I can't sleep. Charles and I took the test this evening, and my mind is just racing." Stacey was smiling from ear to ear. She leaned back in the chair and continued to talk about the baby, clothes, nursery, and anything else having to do with a baby they could come up with.

"You know, when I was pregnant with Riley, there was a part of me that was shut down and off limits," Stacey said as she thought back to her pregnancy.

"Um-hm. I know, Sunshine."

"Well, now that I've gone through this healing process, I already feel a clear difference in this pregnancy. I am ready to live my life free of hidden hurts and bitterness." Stacey felt as though she was on top of the world.

"Well, I would say you need to focus on getting that book published so you can start planning for our new bundle of joy," her mother nudged.

"I agree! I'm going to sneak back to bed now. I'll call you tomorrow, okay?" Stacey whispered.

"Okay, baby. I love you, Sunshine, and I'm so very proud of you," her mother said before she hung up the phone.

Stacey heeded her mother's words and immediately began to work with her editor to finish the book. She decided to use an online company to self-publish the book and submitted her story. About two months went by before the final product was complete.

"Mom, wake up! It's here!" Riley jumped up and down on Stacey's bed.

"Huh, Riley? I'm sleeping. Can it wait?" Stacey mumbled from beneath the covers.

"Your book is here, Mom! You have to get up. You have to see!" Riley stood there waving the book in her hand.

Stacey suddenly had a burst of energy and shot up from the bed. "What! It's here? Let me have that!" she said, reaching out.

Riley handed the book to her mother and plopped down beside her. As Stacey ran her hands down the cover of the book, her heart began to race. She opened the book slowly as she looked at the words on the pages. She flipped the pages and took a deep breath to smell the aroma of fresh print that saturated the air.

"I feel like I'm dreaming, Riley. I've been working so long and hard for this, and here it is. I mean, I went through so much to get here, and this is just the beginning. I can't wait to show Daddy when he gets home." She looked up from the book at Riley with tears in her eyes.

"Mom, you've been crying a lot lately with this baby and everything, but . . . I think this time you *should* cry. I'm proud of you. Maybe one day I can write a book with you." Riley smiled as she leaned her head on Stacey's shoulder.

"Oh, baby. You are the sweetest girl in the world. I would love to write a book with you one day." Stacey put the book down on the bed and hugged Riley.

As they sat on the bed, the phone rang. Stacey reached over on the nightstand and picked up the phone. "Hello?"

"Stacey? This is Heather. Did you get the book yet?" Stacey's editor asked.

"Did I? I love it! It's more than I ever dreamed it would be. It's . . . it's a miracle, Heather. It really is."

"Well, I'm glad to hear it. Hey, I've been shopping your book around to some of my friends to get some feedback. I don't usually do this, but I've been so enamored with your book, and I know how hard it is when you self-publish."

"That's awesome, Heather. I really appreciate that. Hopefully someone likes it as much as you do," Stacey said excitedly.

"Someone does. I have a bookstore owner who wants to order books for his store."

"What?" Stacey jumped out of the bed.

"What, Mom? What's going on?" Riley asked as she knelt on the bed.

Stacey covered the phone with her hand. "Ms. Heather got my book into a bookstore." She walked over to the couch and sat down.

"Heather, I . . . I don't know what to say. I'm honored and surprised because I wasn't expecting this. I wasn't quite sure how God was going to market the book, but I never thought this was going to be the route He was going to take," Stacey's voice squeaked with excitement.

"You should be excited. You worked hard, Stacey. Look, I'm going to send you all the information so you can move forward," Heather said.

"No problem with that one. I look forward to talking with you soon," Stacey said. As she put the phone down, she let out a scream and stretched her hands high. "Lord, You are awesome!" Stacey turned to Riley. "Ry Ry, Mommy is a published author!" She ran over to Riley to hug her.

"Wow, Mom, I guess you can be cool sometimes," Riley teased.

"Why, thank you. I'm so glad I'm moving up in the world," Stacey said, laughing.

Later that evening, Charles and Stacey were lying in bed and talking about the book. It was all sinking in for Stacey, and she was starting to feel a bit scared about what it all meant.

"What do I do next? And what if nobody buys the book?" Stacey just kept asking the questions, not waiting for the answer.

"Stace, you're scared, and that's okay. But you can't believe that God would grant you all this favor and then leave you hanging, right? I know it seems overwhelming, but just get back to the book. You lived this book, so there are no integrity issues. I'm sure we can do some marketing to let people know the book is there." Charles stroked her hair as she rested her head on his chest. "Aren't you one of the top executives at an advertising agency?"

"Yeah, I guess you're right." Stacey closed her eyes.

"Not 'I guess.' You should know I'm right. Do we have to recap this last year for you? You really pushed to get this book finished by using what happened to Kelly as a positive motivating factor and not a crutch. So do that. Remember how your second wind came in this whole process and kept riding it out?" Charles asked.

"You're right. Part of this is for Kelly. There are people out there who feel like she did, and they need to hear what I have to say." Stacey sat up and looked at Charles. "See, that's why I love you. You always know what I need to hear."

"Well, if you love me, don't just tell me, girl. Show me," Charles smiled.

"Okay, if that's what you want," Stacey said, leaning in to give him a kiss.

CHAPTER 15

Stacey followed through with the information Heather gave her, and soon her book was placed on the bookshelf of an independently owned shop in downtown Chicago. The shop was small and quaint and situated on the corner of a busy street. As Stacey walked in, it smelled of books and coffee and looked like a small library. She made her way to the area of the store where her book was. She squinted her eyes as she read the titles of the books that surrounded hers. When she came to her book, she stopped and reached out to touch it.

As she stared at the book, a voice said beside her, "Are you going to get it?"

"Hmm?" Stacey turned her head to see the face that went with the elderly voice standing beside her. "Oh, no. That's a book I've written. I was just admiring it on the shelf. This is my first book," she smiled.

"Oh, my! Well, good for you, young lady." She nodded approvingly.

"Thank you." Stacey felt awkward as the conversation faded. "Um, well, it's been nice speaking with you." She turned and walked to the back of the store to talk to the owner.

"Did you get her to buy your book?" he asked.

"No, I was just telling her it was my book, but that was it. Henry, I don't know what I'm doing." Stacey raised her eyebrows and shrugged.

"It's all about sales, Stacey. In this last month I've talked with you often, and you seem like a very wise woman. Didn't you say you worked for an advertising agency?" Stacey smiled. "Well then, why can't you take those skills and apply them to your book?" He placed his hand on her shoulder.

Stacey stared at Henry for a moment, and her mind flashed back over the last year of her life. After reflecting a moment, she said, "You know what, Henry? You and my husband are right." She laughed. "He told me the same thing, and I obviously didn't get it until now."

"What are you going to do?" Henry asked. He held up his finger. "Hold that thought. I see a customer who needs help."

Stacey looked around the store and thought about what she could do to promote her book. She was flooded with ideas and headed to the front of the store. "Henry, I'll call you next week. I'm going to do some brainstorming and get back to you." Stacey waved to him as she walked out the door.

"Okay, I'll be here!" Henry waved goodbye.

As Stacey drove home, she called her sister. "Shirley, I need you."

"What's up, sis?"

"I want to do a miniature book tour." Stacey paused.

"A book tour?" Shirley asked. "Aren't book tours for well-known authors? How are you going to do that?"

"I'm going to visit small bookstores and ask the owners if I can set up and display my book. And if I sell any of my books, they can get a portion of my proceeds," Stacey replied.

"Wow, ambitious . . ." Shirley's voice sounded doubtful.

"Okay now, don't go there. We're not going to go down that road today. I just need your support," Stacey said sternly.

"All right. I do think it will be hard, but that doesn't mean you shouldn't try," Shirley said, changing her tone.

"Miracles do happen. My sister has changed. Praise the Lord!" Stacey said jokingly.

"Whatever, Stacey! I'm here for you. I've seen what you went through during this last year, and it has affected me too . . . for the better. Just tell me what you need me to do."

"Thanks, Shirley. I love you, and I'll call you in a few days with some details. Can you come over this weekend and help me?" Stacey asked.

"Of course. I got your back, girl," Shirley said.

"Okay, thanks again." Stacey hung up the phone and screamed with joy.

Over the next few weeks, Stacey made her way to several independently owned bookstores and asked to set up her display. She had a few nos and a few yeses.

Mr. Henry's shop was her first location, and she was excited. She struggled to get in the door with a load of her books.

"Do you need help with that?" Henry asked.

"Oh, thank you. These books are heavy, Henry." Stacey handed him a box of books as she leaned on the table to catch her breath. "I can't tell you how much I appreciate this. I've told everyone I know, so it will be interesting to see how it goes."

Henry bent over to place the box on the floor and pulled one out as he stood back up. "Here." He handed it to Stacey.

"What's this for?" she asked.

"Can you sign it for me?" Henry smiled.

"Most certainly!" Stacey fumbled through her purse to find her marker. "You must really be saying that this is going to go well."

"Absolutely. I know it will. Heather has had nothing but great things to say about you and this book. And once I read it, I felt the same way." He pulled out his wallet and placed his money on the table. "Your first sale of the day."

Stacey finished signing his book. "Thank you for giving me a chance." She handed him the book as she fought back tears. "I'm going to finish setting up before people start coming in." Stacey moved on.

"You're more than welcome, Mrs. Brighton." Henry smiled as he walked away. Stacey set up her book flyer on an easel, covered the table with a tablecloth, stacked her books, laid out her markers for signing, and sat down in the chair behind the table. She stared at the front door, waiting for it to open. She sat there for a few minutes as her foot tapped nervously. She stood up and walked over to the door and looked outside. The street was empty.

"They're coming, Stacey," Henry called out behind her.

"Oh, yeah, I know . . . I was just . . . um . . ." Stacey stuttered. She turned around and slowly walked back to her chair. A few moments later the door opened, and a mother and daughter walked in the store. Stacey smiled and tried to make eye contact with them. They smiled and walked past her display. Stacey frowned and put her chin in her hand. She pulled out her journal and began to write. The door opened again, but she didn't look up for fear of another embarrassing moment.

"Excuse me? Can you tell me what this book is about?" a voice said.

"Well—" Stacey started to speak as she looked up. "Charlene! Hey, girl!" Stacey jumped up and ran around the table to hug her friend. "I'm so glad you're here. I'm so nervous."

"I had to be here and see my friend hold it down, and especially with Charles out of town, I knew you needed my support. Can I be your groupie?" Charlene put her hands on her hips.

"Oh please, Charlene. You're crazy." Stacey shoved Charlene and walked back to her chair.

"How many books do you want?" Stacey asked as she handed Charlene a book.

"Oh, I just came to say hey and see how you were doing. I don't want a book."

"Oh, you're going to buy a book . . . maybe three." Stacey pushed the book into Charlene's hands. The ladies let out a hearty laugh.

As they were laughing, they were interrupted. "You're back?"

Stacey heard a voice but didn't see anyone. "Did you hear someone?" she asked Charlene.

"Yes, that was me." A woman peeked her head from behind Charlene.

"Oh, hi. I saw you in here a few weeks ago," Stacey said as she recognized the elderly woman.

"Yes, and I see you're back selling some more books. You know, I bought your book that day," she said as she walked closer to the table.

"You did?" Stacey asked.

"Yes. I read it and felt like you were looking into my life. It was just amazing, and I thank you for your words."

"Wow!" Stacey sat down in the chair. "I'm speechless."

"So you're signing books today?" The woman pointed to the stack of books.

"Yes, I'm trying to do some marketing and let people know about my book," Stacey said.

"Well, I would love to purchase another one for my daughter. Will you sign it for her?" she said as she reached for a book.

"Of course. I'd be honored to do that for you. I appreciate your encouragement." Stacey picked up a pen and took the top off.

"I told my pastor about the book, and I was actually coming in today to ask Henry to do me a favor." She reached out and grabbed Stacey's hand.

"Oh, a favor?" Stacey looked down at her hand.

"Yes. I would like for you to come to my church and speak about your book. There are so many broken and hurting people who need to hear what you have to say."

Stacey looked up at Charlene with excitement. "You want me to come to your church and speak? Wow, I . . . I . . ." Stacey was at a loss for words. She was immediately overwhelmed with fear and doubt as she began to think.

"She would love to," Charlene interrupted.

Stacey shot an evil eye at Charlene. She pulled her hand away from the woman and sat silently for a few moments.

Charlene walked around the table to Stacey and knelt down. "Stacey, this is what you wanted. The book is awesome, and people need to hear your testimony."

When Stacey grimaced, the woman said, "Yes, your testimony. It seemed like there was so much more you had to say as I was reading, sweetheart. Don't you want to share?"

Stacey looked at Charlene and smiled. "Yes, wherever God leads me to speak and share about this book, I will go. I was just a bit taken aback, because this is all happening so fast."

"Oh, I understand, baby. Following after God can be scary, but one thing you can rest assured of is that He will never leave you or let you fall." She picked up Stacey's business card off the table. "Is this how I can reach you?"

"Yes, ma'am. Just let me know the day and time, and I'll be there." Stacey stood up and walked over to the woman. "Thank you very much."

"No—thank you. I'm so excited!" she said as she handed Stacey the money for the book. "Talk to you soon, dear." She took her book and walked out of the store.

As the woman reached the door, Stacey shouted, "Wait! I never got your name."

She turned around and said, "Mrs. Turner . . . Mrs. Kelly Turner." She waved goodbye and left the store. Charlene and Stacey looked at each other and let out a scream.

"Whatever you need, I'm here for you, girl. If you want me to hold your Bible and notes and then put them up on the pulpit for you, I will." Charlene walked over to Stacey.

"You'll be my armor bearer?" Stacey said.

"Yes, your armor bearer . . . wait, you are a tad bit bossy, so maybe I should just play that one by ear." Charlene laughed as she threw her arms around Stacey.

"As long as you're there, Charlene, as long as you're there." Stacey hugged her friend tightly.

The rest of her time at the bookstore was filled with many candid conversations with customers, book signings, and sales. She ended the day feeling more confident than ever before. She had three more book signings over the next few weeks, and all of them were successful, which led to her book being carried in all of the stores she visited.

The time came a few months later for her to speak at Mrs. Turner's church. Stacey sat on the couch in her bedroom and rubbed her stomach as she felt her baby moving. She opened her journal. As she looked out of the window, she saw the leaves starting to change colors. "Fall is here already," she said softly. She looked down and rubbed her hand over the blank page in her journal. Slowly she took the pen in her hand and began to write.

I am here only by the grace of God. What can I say? I have been healed, delivered, and set free.

She laughed out loud as she wrote the sentence.

It sounds like a cliché, but it's real. You saved me, God. I am overwhelmed with appreciation and gratitude. To be able to walk in my purpose and be transparent without fear is such a gift. I have to admit I'm nervous about today, but I'm equally excited. I want someone to feel what I am feeling.

A tear fell onto the page, smearing the ink of her words. Stacey closed her journal and laid it beside her. She leaned over, rested her head on the pillow, and began to cry.

"Knock, knock?" Shirley stood in the doorway of her room.

"Oh, come on in," Stacey said as she sat up and wiped her face.

"Are you okay, sis?" Shirley walked into the room and sat down next to Stacey.

"Yes, I was just reflecting on all that God has done in this last year and how . . . how blessed I am." Stacey leaned her head on Shirley's shoulder.

"That you are. And we, your family, are blessed as well. But you have no idea how many more people are going to blessed when you share your testimony today, including that unborn child in there." She wrapped her arm around Stacey's waist and placed her other hand on Stacey's stomach.

"Oh, my goodness!" Stacey jumped up. "What time is it?"

"Calm down. We have time. I just came upstairs to tell you we're leaving in forty-five minutes, so get dressed." Shirley stood up and took hold of Stacey's hand.

"Oh, thanks. I'll be down shortly." Stacey smiled.

"Okay, lady, let's go, Shirley teased as she stood up and walked out of the room.

Stacey took her time to get dressed. She eyed herself in the mirror and practiced what she was going to say a few times. As she left the bathroom to head downstairs, she looked at her laptop on the desk in front of her window. She walked over to it and closed her eyes as she touched the computer. *"This is for you, Kelly."* She touched her chest over her heart before she turned toward the door.

The drive to the church was quiet as she read her Bible and prayed silently. Riley sat quietly in the back seat while Charles hummed softly in the driver's seat. She walked into the church and let out a gasp when she entered the sanctuary.

"Wow, this is a huge church, Mom." Riley stole the words from Stacey.

"Yes, sweetie, it is," Stacey replied as she scanned the pews and the balcony.

"Stacey!" Mrs. Turner called from across the room.

Stacey smiled and felt a warmth come over her as she walked toward the friendly face. "Hello, Mrs. Turner. It's so nice to see you." Stacey held out her hand.

"No, we hug here, sweetheart," she said as she drew Stacey into her arms. "Well, you're just in time because we're going to get started shortly. Follow me to your seat." She tugged Stacey's arm.

"Oh, I can just sit with my family. I don't need—" Stacey pulled away.

Mrs. Turner looked Stacey in the eye. "Now shuga, you're going to have to embrace this a hundred percent. Let your gift make room for you." She winked. "Stretch out a little."

Stacey reluctantly followed Mrs. Turner to the front of the church while Charles, Riley, Shirley, and her family sat a few rows behind her. A few minutes later, as the service began, she turned around and saw Charlene walking in. Stacey smiled and glanced at Charles who nodded. "I love you," she whispered. As she waited to be introduced, she prayed silently.

Lord, I know You set me on this path, and therefore, You got me. I will enjoy this and lay down every single fear I'm feeling at this very moment. Let the people hear You and not me. I sure do love You today, Jesus. Amen.

Stacey heard her name called, and she smiled nervously as she stood up to walk to the stage. She let out a long slow breath as she reached the podium and began to lay out her notes and her Bible. Her heart was beating so hard that she thought everyone could see it through her dress. As she looked out into the congregation, she made eye contact with Charlene, who waved frantically and took out a tissue. Stacey laughed as she opened her Bible. She took a moment to compose herself and then opened her mouth to speak. She felt as though she was a diver jumping into the deep end of the pool.

"Good morning. First of all, I would like to thank Mrs. Turner for inviting me and Pastor Levings for allowing me in his pulpit. About a year ago God called me to write a book. I was excited and scared at the same time. I really got scared when I realized all that I was going to have to endure, face, and reveal throughout the writing process." Stacey began to feel goose bumps as the words flowed and the people appeared engaged.

She continued, "God calls us to do many things. He says to forgive, love, be patient with each other, and give to each other. It all begins with grace though, right?"

She heard some amens from the audience.

"It was by His grace that He saved us, and it is by grace that we are able to do all of these things He has called us to do. But, if we are honest with ourselves, the truth is these things can be very difficult to do at times, especially when you're dealing with people whom you believe are unforgivable, unlovable, and greedy."

Stacey took a deep breath. "Well, let me tell you what I learned *after* I began writing this book. The key to your success is . . . The Mercy of Humanity."

ABOUT THE AUTHOR

S HANTE CARTER, now a published author, is also
an independent recording artist, accountant, wife,
and mother. She is excited about sharing her gifts and
talents with any and everyone who will listen. Shante
and her husband, Aaron, reside in Windsor Mill,
Maryland, and have two wonderful children.

ORDER INFO.

To order *The Mercy of Humanity*
for yourself, a friend, or family member,
contact the author or order from your favorite bookseller.
Bulk discounts are available from the publisher.

For autographed books,
to schedule speaking engagements,
or to ask questions, contact:

Shante Carter
PO Box 2523
Ellicott City, MD 21041-2523
purposed4life@gmail.com

———————————

Fruitbearer Publishing, LLC
P. O. Box 777, Georgetown, DE 19947
302.856.6649 • FAX 302.856.7742
info@fruitbearer.com
www.fruitbearer.com